Alfred Rochefort Calhoun

Kohala of Hawaii

A Story of the Sandwich Islands Revolution

Alfred Rochefort Calhoun

Kohala of Hawaii
A Story of the Sandwich Islands Revolution

ISBN/EAN: 9783743400160

Manufactured in Europe, USA, Canada, Australia, Japa

Cover: Foto ©Andreas Hilbeck / pixelio.de

Manufactured and distributed by brebook publishing software (www.brebook.com)

Alfred Rochefort Calhoun

Kohala of Hawaii

BY
ALFRED R. CALHOUN

———————

Specially written for " Once a Week Library"

———————

NEW YORK
PETER FENELON COLLIER
1893

KOHALA OF HAWAII.

INTRODUCTION.

No ALIEN land in all the world has so strong an attraction, so profound a charm for the American who has trod its emerald shores, as beautiful "Hawaii"—the native, and hence the proper, name for what Captain Cook, their discoverer, called the "Sandwich Islands." Sleeping or waking, how lovingly its beauties haunt me as I, fresh from its ever-blooming gardens and ever-burning volcanoes, sit down to write, from a heart that is full of it, the story of the last great drama enacted in that fair land, for whose possession the maritime nations of the world are intriguing to-day.

CHAPTER I.

THE PARADISE OF THE PACIFIC.

Two MILES back from the capital city of Honolulu there rises an extinct volcano, known far and near as the "Punch Bowl," and accessible from the town by a fine road.

People in carriages, well-mounted equestrians and energetic pedestrians usually swarm about the Punch Bowl's rugged crest when the sun is setting, for then the ocean breeze is always cool and refreshing, and from Diamond

(3)

Head, to the east, to Pearl Harbor, on the west, there is
such a panorama of exquisite beauty spread out before
the observer as entrances newcomers and gives a never-
ceasing delight to those who have seen it before.

The short twilight of the tropics was fading over Honolulu, but this evening the Punch Bowl appeared to be
deserted, no doubt because the black cloud banners that
threatened one of those brief but violent storms peculiar
to these islands streamed out from Diamond Head and
veiled the Pali's bloody cliff. The pulsating glow of sheet
lightning illuminated these clouds, and a hoarse grum-
bling came down from the mountains to the garden-
embowered city by the sea.

From the jungle of lantana, that clothes the Punch
Bowl from base to crest, two young men, with a backward glance to make sure their horses were secure,
walked out to the circular protecting wall around the
summit. That they were men of nerve, or so familiar
with the scene that they had a contempt for its dangers,
was shown by the fact that they sat down on the wall,
nor seemed to give thought to the fact that a stone, loosened by one as he adjusted himself to the place, plunged
down for eight hundred feet of nearly precipitous descent.

Both these young men were dressed after the fashion of
horsemen in Hyde Park, the Bois de Boulogne or Cen-
tral Park. One was short, stout, blue-eyed, and had the
florid face and thick neck which are usually found associated with men who know no enjoyment beyond those
of the senses. Yet there was a set to the jaws, an expression about the chin and a certain firmness in his bearing that denoted force and had in it the suggestion of a
military training.

The other man, although not above medium height, looked taller, because of his slender, erect figure and a certain easy, tigerish grace in his movements that indicated a rare union of strength and activity. The long black hair, the well-cut, olive features, the gleaming white teeth, and the dark eyes, that seemed to glow as if with an internal light, told that the man, whose age could not have been more than five-and-twenty, was a native, but a native of higher type and finer fiber than the average people of his race.

One by one, from amid the groves of palm and crimson hybiscus, the lights in Honolulu became visible, and the breakers that had seemed, as the man advanced to the wall, like rising and fading lines of snow on the shore became banks of liquid fire—never seen outside the tropics— banks that glowed with a strange, green, phosphorescent light, suggestive of cold rather than heat, like the flashing of the aurora borealis on an arctic wintry night.

That these men had not come up to view the scenery was shown by the fact that they did not look at it, but sat on the wall for some minutes without speaking, each appearing to be wrapped in his own thoughts and in the contemplation of the other's face.

Captain Paul Featherstone, the white man, was the first to break the silence. Speaking in accents that un mistakably bespoke his English nationality, and that indicated association with cultured people if not culture itself, he said:

"Kohala, I agree with you that the time is ripe for action. Since we first met, when you were studying in Paris two years ago, my faith in your claims to the throne of Hawaii and my appreciation of your fitness for the position have grown stronger and stronger. But

I would be a fool and not your friend if I closed my eyes to the difficulties that beset you—that beset us—for I have linked my fate with yours. Now that we are on the ground, we find a queen on the throne, whom your countrymen regard as legitimate, and with Americans among her advisers; but she is too blind to see that they are planning to depose her and to make Hawaii a part of their overgrown republic."

Kohala, the young Hawaiian, tossed over the battlement a fragment of rock with which he had been toying and responded in tones that indicated impatience.

"I still think, Captain Featherstone, that you continue to misunderstand me."

"In what way?" asked the captain, in surprise.

"In this way: Have I not proven clearly to you and to other friends that I, as the known, though as yet unrecognized, only male descendant of the great King Kamehameha, am the rightful sovereign of Hawaii?"

"Unmistakably," replied the captain, in a voice that showed he considered this settled beyond the possibility of doubt.

"And have I not also told you and other friends that personally I cared nothing for the throne, that indeed I was not a believer in the divine right or any other right of kings, that I was and am at heart a republican?" said Kohala, in a voice raised above the previous key, but which only served the more to bring out its melody and to show that he loved to dwell on vowel sounds, but had no fondness for the harsher consonants that distinguish our Northern speech.

"Surely, you have told me all that," replied the captain, "and, as your friend, I have not hesitated to oppose your views. I am an Englishman, and so believe in kings, and queens, too, and so do not believe in the license of republics, such as we see in that overgrown monster to the east, through which you and I recently traveled."

"Captain Featherstone," said Kohala, in graver accents and with his fine, expressive face upraised to the lowering clouds, "I must still cling to my opinion about kings."

"And give up your claims to the throne?"

"A man is not fit to be a king whom his people, if left free to choose, would not select for a ruler. I have traveled through many lands, and my heart has bled at the vice, the poverty and the degradation that seem inseparable from civilization where kings rule, and to some extent in modern republics; but it is from this that I would save the remnant of my race. A century ago we numbered nearly half a million; to-day we are barely forty thousand. We have had kings and queens in Hawaii since and before the time of Cook's unfortunate discovery. Yet the work of civilization, of your civilization (?) goes on. The missionary is here, but so is the liquor seller; and the adventurer who has seized on our most beautiful valleys, and forced into the volcanic hills the natives who will not work in his sugar and coffee fields. I believe that the God of the white man is the God of the Hawaiian, and that He never meant that we should be destroyed, and that a race that worships only wealth and the power it represents should send us to the grave and erect their palaces where we were once so happy. I want to arouse the people to a sense of their duty. I want to show them that a descendant of the great king who united them is ready to lead them in the assertion of their rights, and that he is willing to die for them, if his death will accomplish the purpose that is so near and so dear to his heart, and that fills him and thrills him, whether sleeping or waking."

"All this is noble," said the Englishman, "but is it practical?"

"Whatever is right must be made practical," replied Kohala, with spirit.

"True; still we must take things as they are and not as we would have them." Then with a forced laugh that indicated his feelings and character more than anything he said, Captain Featherstone added: "We live in a practical age—an age of selfishness, when dreamers are laughed at or forced to the wall. My country, England, has flourished because she realizes that material prosperity is the only foundation of success. If you see fit to adopt her methods, as I have told you before, you will find her a friend. She can place you on the throne and keep you on it, but it will be necessary for you to follow her instructions—"

"And to be her tool—her slave?" broke in Kohala.

"No; to be her ally and her friend. Republics may foster slaves; it is England's boast that every man breathing the air protected by her flag is a free man. But a storm threatens, let us be getting back. And then, I think the queen will be disappointed if you are not at the ball to-night."

"She would rather see me there dead than alive," said Kohala, and, as he arose from the wall, another stone was loosened and went thundering into the valley in the direction of Honolulu.

"And the beautiful widow, Mrs. Holmes. Don't you think she will miss you if you are absent from the palace to-night?" laughed the Englishman, as they turned in the direction of the horses.

"Would the sun miss one of the smaller planets that circle about it, seen only by its light? No; I might miss the face of the fair Englishwoman from the scene, but amid so many admirers, men of her own race, Marguerite Holmes could hardly be aware that Kohala, the Kanaka pretender, was present or absent."

This was said with some bitterness, yet there was that in the young prince's accents, and particularly in the caressing way in which he pronounced the lady's name, that told he did not regard her as an ordinary mortal.

By the time the two men were in the saddle the storm that had been gathering about the mountains to the north burst upon the Punch Bowl and shut out the myriad electric lamps that had been glowing with a cold white light in the direction of Honolulu.

The winding road from the crest of the hill was unobstructed and of easy descent, and the horses were eager to be back in their stalls, so the riders gave them free rein, and flew down to the line at a gallop, which was maintained till they swept into grounds illuminated by lamps and the light coming through the windows of a broad, low building, about which ran a wide piazza, such as is peculiar to the better class of houses in Honolulu.

As the riders dismounted two native men appeared to take the horses, and the salaams and salutations of love and respect with which they greeted Kohala showed that he had at least two strong adherents in the capital of Hawaii.

CHAPTER II.

THE BALL AT THE PALACE.

SET amid groves of palms and surrounded by parterres of ever-blooming flowers, the national palace at Honolulu, with its stately architecture and its indications of refined taste and exquisite luxury. presents a pleasing picture when seen under the blaze of the midday sun. At all hours a native soldier, in a white uniform, paces on guard before the cataract of marble steps leading up to the grand entrance hall, and this adds to the air of exclusiveness that seems to bar the structure from the outside world, as a great wall might not do.

But beautiful and inviting though the palace is in the golden sunlight, it becomes doubly so at night, when Queen Liliuokalini (pronounced Lily-wak-a-lee-nee) gives a *fete champetre*, a band concert or a ball. On such occasions the palace is all aglow with light, and the great doors and windows are opened to permit it to pour out in soft golden streams. The cunning of the Chinese gardeners is invoked, and a wonderful transformation is effected. Tiny fairy-lamps are concealed so skillfully among the flower-banks that each blossom seems to glow with its own light. Like luminous fruit, colored lamps flash amid the graceful fronds of the towering palms, and arches of colored lights span the winding walks, and festoons of lights, like vines of iridescent flame, link the trees and dazzle the sight of the beholder.

Behind a screen of flowering cacti and plumelike

ferns the Queen's band is concealed on these festive
occasions, but this serves but to increase the effect of
the music that fills the palace halls, and sets the light
feet of the pleasure-seekers a-moving, and forces the walk
of the promenaders into a dancing measure, till even the
most prosaic feels that he has left the harsh, materialistic
world behind him and is transported to fairyland.

Newcomers to Hawaii, who had been honored by an
invitation to the Queen's ball to-night, feared that the
storm that burst on the city after sunset would interfere
with the attendance, or at least with the pleasure of the
occasion; but the older residents, who knew how brief
these storms were, laughed at their fears, and declared
that the rain would add to the attractiveness of the ball,
by laying the dust and cooling the air; and they were
right.

By nine o'clock that evening the sky was as clear as
if it had never floated a raincloud. The moon and the
larger stars shone down with a brilliancy unknown in
higher latitudes; and from over the coral barrier reef
there came the droning sound of the breakers, lulling
the city to sleep. But to the gay throngs in and about
the palace the night would be all too short, nor would
the morning be welcome that brought repose.

From long lines of carriages, ladies and gentlemen in
evening dress, and of all nationalities, descended and
poured up the great stairs to the apartments where
attendants took charge of their wraps, then came down
to the drawing-room to pay their respects to the Queen,
who, surrounded by her maids of honor, received them
with graciousness and dignity, some of which was natural, but much more of which was assumed.

The Queen's dazzling evening dress served to make

more pronounced the more than becoming plumpness
of her figure, while it intensified the darkness of her
complexion. The full, sensuous lips and a certain indescribable coquetry in her manner, which was particularly perceptible when she was talking to gentlemen,
told that fifty-two years, while they might have left silver streaks in the regal dowager's hair, had not weakened her opinion of her powers to captivate.

Queen Liliuokalani's maids of honor on this occasion
were, with two exceptions, Hawaiians. With more
adroitness, or less faith in her own simple but anti-
quated charms, the Queen might have selected young
women whose beauty was less pronounced; but she had
not done so. The exquisite olive faces, framed in masses
of dark hair, rendered blacker and more luminous by intertwined crimson blossoms, the finely molded arms
and busts and the lithe, graceful forms of the Hawaiian
maids of honor were well calculated to withdraw from
Her Majesty the admiring glances of the uniformed
officers and foreign representatives who attended the
ball.

It has been said that two of the maids of honor, though
their position as such was only for this evening, were not
natives. One of these was a beautiful American girl,
Alice Ellis, the daughter of one of the richest sugar
planters on the island, and the other was an Englishwoman, who at the first glance did not seem to be a
person who could attract much attention; this was
"Mrs. Marguerite Holmes," as her cards indicated.

Mrs. Marguerite Holmes had been in Honolulu less
than a year. She had left England for California some
eighteen months before this, in the hope of restoring the
health of her husband, Professor Holmes, who, it was

said, contracted, from overstudy at Oxford, the disease
which sent him to the grave before he had been a month
at Los Angeles. When, soon after her husband's death,
Mrs. Holmes came to Hawaii, and said it was for her
health, no one was inclined to dispute her, for she was
frail to emaciation, and she had such an innocent, girlish expression and was so unworldly as to call for the
protection of strong men, and, at first, for the sympathy
of her own sex.

If Mrs. Holmes's most ardent admirer—and it will be
seen that she had many such—were asked if she were
beautiful the unhesitating answer would be "No." If
asked if she were pretty, the answer would be varied
and qualified; but if asked if she were attractive, and
particularly to men who imagined they had reached
years of discretion, it would be generally conceded that
she was decidedly so. But as she was neither intellect
ual nor accomplished, though unmistakably well bred,
her most ardent advocate—and she needed such—would
be at a loss to tell in what she excelled or why he was
drawn so irresistibly to her.

Mrs. Holmes was of medium height, and so slender
as to seem angular in contrast with the superbly formed
women about her. Her neck was thin, but this, like
every other physical defect, was concealed by the skill
of her comparatively plain yet perfectly arranged attire.
Her finely formed head was covered by a coil of silky,
gold-bronze hair, that glistened with a rich metallic
sheen under the lights. Over the forehead the wavy
fringe looked very much darker and suggested to the
trained eye the ravages of the curling-iron. The forehead was low, but fairly broad and full over the temples.
The eyebrows were unusually thick, meeting over a by

no means classic nose. and they looked black in contrast with the hair. The eyes, long-lashed and gray, and with an expression that momentarily changed from girlish coyness to skilled coquetry, were the redeeming feature of the face. The complexion was pale, the mouth almost childish in its pouting uncertainty, and the chin far from indicating strength. Yet, taken as a whole, and particularly when animated, Mrs. Holmes looked like an innocent, captivating girl of nineteen, though she confessed to being twenty-six.

This was the woman about whom all Honolulu was now talking, some in unmistakable laudation and others in doubt and denunciation quite as positive. To some she was a gentle, guileless, charming woman, who needed protection and sympathy: to others she was a heartless, designing adventurer, if, indeed, she were not something far worse.

The crush of visitors had been received by the Queen, and she was about to withdraw, when the names of Kohala and Captain Paul Featherstone were announced. Barely bowing to the Englishman, who at once drew Mrs. Holmes to one side and entered into earnest conversation with her, the Queen gave her young countryman her hand, which he did not kiss, as the others had done, and said in good English :

"I feared, my cousin, that you would not honor us to-night?"

"I was caught in the storm," he said, "but I am too good a Hawaiian not to regard as a command the invitation of our Queen."

"I might, indeed, believe your presence a compliment and an indication of your loyalty did I not fear that another and a more powerful attraction than myself brought you to the palace to-night." Here the Queen smiled and inclined her head toward Mrs. Holmes; then before the young man could recover from his evident confusion and reply, she added: "But as we can talk again this evening, I shall not detain you. I fully appreciate your eagerness to be with another."

With this sally Her Majesty waved her hand, and, followed by nearly all her maids, left the drawing-room.

One of the girls, who remained back, was a Hawaiian of not more than seventeen. She was a lithe, beautiful girl, with a face as perfect as ever sculptor's chisel formed, and eyes such as never a painter transferred to canvas. This girl was Leila, daughter of Keona, a renowned prince or chief of the great fire island of Hawaii, to the southeast of Oahu, on which Honolulu is situated.

As Kohala moved in the direction of Mrs. Holmes he felt a light touch on his arm, and turning, with the quick start of one rudely aroused from a dream, he saw the beautiful Leila standing with drooping head beside him.

Taking her hand, after a pause, like one obeying a second impulse, Kohala said:

"Leila, I did not expect to see you here. When did you leave your father, and how did you leave him?"

"I left him well, two days ago," she replied. Then in a voice sunk to a flutelike whisper: "I bear you a message from my father, Kohala, and must see you to-night."

"I shall find you within the hour," was his response.

Leila followed in the direction the Queen had taken, but Kohala did not see that as she passed out her left hand was pressed to her heart, as if to still a pain.

The instant Captain Featherstone saw the young Hawaiian approaching he turned to Mrs. Holmes, gave her a meaning glance and then moved off toward the dancers.

Kohala was evidently confused, and hesitated for a second as he held Mrs. Holmes's ungloved hand, but with grace and tact, and one of those arch smiles that were the strongest weapons in her armory, she said:

"I have been standing here looking for you all evening, Kohala, and now that you have rested my heart by coming I want you to take me to a place where I can rest my feet and we can talk without being disturbed."

"When you so well express my wishes," he said, with a pleased smile and a blush that lighted up his olive face, "there is no need for me to talk; indeed, I never can talk when you are near me. At such times I am quite content and happy in looking and watching."

"And in coining princely compliments," she said, with the slightest additional pressure on the arm she had taken and a glance through those wonderful long lashes that would have been potent with a more experienced man than Kohala.

The Queen's enemies, and there were many such, wondered why he had taken such a fancy to the young English widow, and some thought they saw in it an indication of England's secret diplomacy; while still others shrugged their shoulders and whispered the old adage: "Birds of feather flock together." And now as Kohala made his way to the gardens, evidently unconscious of everything but the slender, girlish figure by his side, men and women of both parties and all parties looked after them, and there were meaning nods and winks; and one lady, speaking with a decided New England accent, said to her escort:

"Well, she has a fine selection of sweethearts. To my

certain knowledge she is leading an old Mormon priest who lives near here to believe she is in love with him; and one of her greatest admirers, a young fellow who felt he must wear good clothes to stand well with her, was arrested a few days since for forgery. Old or young, black or white, she doesn't seem to care so that he's a man easily led and ready to be fooled. Bah! I loathe women of that class; they foster scandal and breed divorces!"

At the further end of the grounds from the palace there was and is a little summer-house, where at times the Queen retires when she wishes to be undisturbed. To-night, with the moonlight sifting through the tangle of vines and falling on the broad rustic seat, it was an ideal place for lovers.

To this place Kohala escorted Mrs. Holmes, and when they were seated he still retained her hand. It was steady and cool, and his trembled and was feverish.

"Ah, with you by my side, Kohala," she said, with a touch on his arm that thrilled him, "this is far more delightful than the crowd, of which I have a horror, or the dancing, for which I never care—unless I can select my own partner, and as yet the world has not advanced enough to give us poor women that privilege."

"The world will soon be advanced enough," said Kohala, "to give to every human being every right that God intended that his children should enjoy—"

"Oh, now you are going to talk about liberty, and all that; things that I do not understand," she said, poutingly.

"No," he responded, "to-night I am going to talk of something that you, more than any woman I ever met, should understand perfectly."

"Oh, Kohala, you frighten me!" she said, as she drew nearer to him in her winning, childlike fashion, and clung to his arm as if to be protected from himself. Then, as if reassured by the contact: "But go on, and tell me what this subject is."

"It is love!" he said, and he bent over her till she must have felt his hot breath on her cheek.

"Love?" she repeated, questioningly.

"Yes, love; my love! But why should I tell you that of which your own heart must have convinced you, Marguerite?"

"Do not call me 'Mârguerite'; those who like me call me Flossy," she said.

"Flossy let it be! Flossy, you know how I love you! You know that I have one great purpose in life, a purpose for which I would give my life! Yet you are nearer and dearer than that. Now give me the answer for which my heart has hungered since first we met!"

His arms were about her, and she made a faint effort to avoid the torrent of kisses which he rained on her face, that was never for an instant averted.

At length, though it may have been because of a rustle in the vines near by, he released her, and gasped:

"Now give me my answer! Do you love me?"

"I love you as I never loved man before," she replied.

"And you will be my wife? my queen?"

"Do not ask me that now. You must have patience. Wait, Kohala, wait till I have had time to think. No, not now!" she said, for she had risen to her feet and he was trying to draw her down to his side. "Let us go back to the palace. I—I am afraid we are watched!"

She had no fear of their being watched, nor did she

suspeet it, as on his arm she returned to the palace, yet such was the case.

It was not to play the spy, but to ease the anguish at her own heart that Leila stole away from her friends in the palace and sought the seclusion of the garden. She was about to enter the summer-house when the low murmur of voices told her it was occupied. Before she could retrace her steps, Kohala and Marguerite Holmes came out, and as they disappeared in the direction of the palace the beautiful girl clung to the arbor for support and sobbed:

"Oh, she is heartless, and her plaything is the most precious thing in life to me!

CHAPTER III.

THE CONSPIRATORS.

"How does she live?" was a question which people skeptical as to Mrs. Holmes often asked each other. The answer was usually an arching of the eyebrows or a shrug of the shoulders. This question applied to the lady's resources and not to the manner of her living. It was well known that with a maid, brought with her from England—this "maid," as her mistress called her, was a taciturn woman of five-and-forty—Mrs. Holmes lived in the one-half of a large furnished cottage, rented from a respectable couple who had more room than they needed.

As Mrs. Holmes neither borrowed nor ran into debt her enemies were disappointed, for from their first dis-

like they had prophesied that she would do both before
long, and that she would skip away on some steamer,
when she was quite ready, and leave her creditors to
curse their credulity.

It was the morning following the Queen's ball, and
those who had attended, and whose duties did not call
them up, were asleep. Mrs. Holmes, dressed in a loose
red wrapper of some soft material that gave by its reflection a becoming glow to her usually pale cheeks,
had had her breakfast by nine o'clock and was out in
the garden attending the flowers, in her great love for
which there certainly was no affectation. Suddenly, she
came upon a lame kitten under the bushes, and though
she had never seen it before, with a cry of mingled pain
and sympathy she caught the little creature up, pressed
it to her breast and ran into her own bedroom, which
opened by swinging windows on the piazza.

"Clem!" she called out—'Clem' was the name by which
she addressed the maid—"run across to Dr. Wallace and
tell him I want him at once!"

Without a word the maid ran out, and Mrs. Holmes
was making the kitten comfortable on a pillow when
a gray-headed man of sixty, with an unmistakable medi-
cal expression, came in. He found Mrs. Holmes actually
crying over the kitten.

"Ah," he said, as he recognized the object of her so-
licitude, "I feared it was yourself, but I see it is my
kitten."

"Then there is all the more reason I should be kind
to it, and that you should cure it," she said, drying her
eyes with one hand and laying the other on his arm.

The doctor was a widower, but the expression in his
eyes, as he turned to the woman, told that his remaining

so would depend enitrely on her. He told her the kitten would soon be all right, adding, as he held her hand before leaving:

"If it should keep ill it will give me a good professional excuse for calling."

She looked at him in a way that said plainer than words: "I shall always be rejoiced to see you."

"They may slander that little widow as they please," said Dr. Wallace to a friend, to whom he related this incident shortly afterward, "but a woman with such a heart and such childlike ways must be an angel."

The doctor had been gone but a few minutes when Clem came into the chamber where her mistress was still fondling the cat and said\ that Captain Featherstone wished to see her in the parlor.

Mrs. Holmes hastily arranged her hair before a mirror, fastened a blue blossom in the high collar of her wrapper and went to see her guest. She gave the captain the same sweet smile she had given the doctor, and her reception was made more pronounced by her extending to him both hands; and, not to be outdone, he raised the hands to his lips and kissed them alternately.

"You have a wonderful constitution," he said, admiringly. "I feared you would be very weary after last night's carouse, but you are as fresh as a daisy. Now sit down, Marguerite—beg pardon, Flossy—and tell me the situation." And the captain placed a chair for her and sat down facing her.

"There is not much to tell at present," she said, with her eyes cast down in a pretty, demure way on her thin, interlocked fingers. "He wants me to marry him, and if I agreed to do that, I am certain he could be made to relinquish his republican notions."

"And why can't you agree? Mind you, I don't say
that you shall marry him, that I could not stand; but
we must be able to lead him. This is the situation : The
natives on the other islands, and many here, believe he is
the rightful heir to the throne of Hawaii, and they are
ready to depose the Queen, if Kohala announces himself. With this young man on the throne, England can
dominate these islands and the Yankees will be beaten
at their own game; for if the adherents of Kohala do
not oust the Queen the Americans will, and once they
hoist their flag here and announce a protectorate they
will be in control, and they will keep it. Success means
a fortune to us, Marguerite, a future and a home in dear
old England. I know it is not in your nature to play a
false part, but for the present you must be an actor and
hold your power over Kohala."

There was evidently a perfect understanding between
these two; certainly the captain believed so. He had
faith in Marguerite Holmes, but then so did any man
who came within reach of her remarkable influence.

While Captain Featherstone was thus working for
England's ends—and his own—by urging his country-
woman to retain her hold on a man he regarded as "a
gilded savage." a number of American representative
merchants and planters were holding what they call
a "caucus", in a guarded room of the Hawaiian Hotel.

Among these Americans were two of the Queen's
cabinet, men who had large interests on the islands.
but who had won the enmity of Her Majesty by their
republican manners and their opposition to what they
very properly regarded as her arbitrary and unconstitutional methods.

One of these gentlemen had just announced that the

Queen, in defiance of established law, was about to promulgate a new constitution, which, if carried into effect, would make American property, which represented eighty per cent. of all the wealth in Hawaii, practically valueless and render the islands unsafe as the abode of any but a native.

"If we do not interfere to stop this," said one of the ministers, "the English will; and once England gets her hands on Hawaii she will not be in a hurry to relinquish her grasp."

Colonel Ellis, a rich planter from the island of Hawaii, and a man whose bearing and manners showed that his military title was not assumed, rose and said in a low-voiced, deliberate way, that was more effective than a vociferous address:

"The natives of Hawaii are as weary of their Queen as ourselves. Yet, they are a proud people and will never be content to have a white man at the head of their affairs, though white men direct them now. I think I see a way to getting rid of the Queen and at the same time placing, as an elected president, a man in the chair who is the rightful heir to the throne, and withal a native, and a young man of ability. When he was a lad, after the manner of these people, particularly the families of chiefs, he was espoused to Leila, daughter of the Chief Keona of Hawaii. If we could bring this marriage about at once, and Kohala, whose heart is wrapped up in the interests of his people, will agree to it, I am sure we can satisfy the natives and have a man in power who, while doing injustice to none, will co-operate with us for the good of all. Indeed, he told me, soon after his return, that under proper conditions he would favor annexation to the States, or such a pro-

tectorate as would take these islands forever out of
the reach of these avaricious European nations, now so
eager to possess them."

"Colonel Ellis," said Mr. George King, a gentleman
interested in the lumber trade between Honolulu and
Puget's Sound, "have you been watching this young
Kohala of late?"

"I have not," was the reply; "but I am quite sure he
is doing nothing that is not right."

"I suppose," laughed Mr. King, "that none of us would
call anything so natural as falling in love, wrong?"

The company laughed, and, to a man, said: "Of course
not."

"But with whom has Kohala fallen in love?" asked
Colonel Ellis.

"I am told on good authority that he is one of the
most devoted admirers of this Englishwoman, Mrs.
Holmes," said Mr. King.

"Mrs. Holmes!" repeated Colonel Ellis.

"Then you have not heard of her? That proves that
you have been away from Honolulu. She is a young
widow, neither rich, talented nor particularly prepos-
sessing, if you come to analyze her, who has half the
men in love with her, and the other half, with about all
the women, denouncing her. Among the women, however, is not Her Majesty, for Mrs. Holmes, with her
peculiarly insinuating ways, has made herself a frequent, and so a welcome, visitor at the palace. Why,
last night, I heard Her Majesty joking the little widow
about Kohala, and the little widow purred in her kit-
tenish way, and looked pleased."

"I see it!" said Colonel Ellis, with unusual energy.
"The Queen wants Kohala to marry a white woman.

That act would kill him with the natives and she knows it. But, surely, the young man is not infatuated with this unknown person?"

"But he is," persisted Mr. King and others.

"Then," said the colonel, "we must act to prevent such an alliance. Either Kohala must give up this woman, or, better still, she must be forced to leave Honolulu."

CHAPTER IV.

THE QUEEN'S PROPOSITION.

OUTSIDE the door of the room in the Hawaiian Hotel, where the Americans were assembled, there was stationed a guard to prevent intrusion, and every man who passed this guard did so by virtue of a pass-word.

During the meeting, fully twenty men were admitted in this way, mostly Americans, but there were not a few German and French merchants among the company, who frankly confessed that they would prefer that Hawaii should belong to their own countries, but who, as this was not feasible, were determined that England should not add these beautiful islands to her vast Polynesian possessions.

These foreigners, if such they can be called, strongly advocated forcing the Queen from the throne, and then asking Captain Wiltze, of the United States warship *Boston*, for American protection. until such times as the leading citizens should decide on a permanent form of government.

In anticipation of just such a movement, Colonel

Ellis had drawn up, before coming to the meeting, a scheme of organization that would insure protection until a convention representative of all interests should decide on annexation to the United States, or to form an independent republic under the protection of that country.

"Before proceeding further, gentlemen," said Colonel Ellis, as he rose with his written scheme in his hand, "I propose, for present secrecy and future success, that we, who are here assembled, subscribe to a pledge in which we shall bind ourselves to keep our own council, and to work without ceasing until our purpose is accomplished. Does this meet with your approval?"

"Ay! Ay! Ay!" burst from every man in the room.

"Then let every man rise, lift his right hand, give his own name, then repeat after me."

Every man rose and raised his right hand, and the expression on the strong, bearded faces showed that they did not regard this act as a theatrical ceremony.

"I, Norman Ellis."

Every man solemnly repeated his own name.

"Of my own free will and accord."

"Of my own free will and accord."

"And in the presence of Almighty God and these witnesses, do solemnly swear that I will never divulge, to one not authorized to receive the same, the names, acts or purposes of this, the Patriotic Council of Hawaii. And, believing that our liberties, if not our property and lives, are threatened by the arbitrary, unconstitutional and barbarous conduct of the Queen, I hereby solemnly pledge myself to use all my best efforts to depose her, by mild means if possible, but by force if need be. And I further promise and swear that I will freely and

promptly obey the orders of the Council, without regard to my own loss of money or time, and that I will
do all in my power to protect the rights of the weakest
and humblest citizen of Hawaii as well as if they were
my own. To all this I pledge my honor as a man
and a citizen. So help me God, and enable me to do
unto others as I would that they should do unto me!"

A solemn silence followed the conclusion of this oath.
Each felt that while it had not strengthened his personal
purpose it united him more closely to men whose interests were common with his own.

Although the law might call these men "conspirators,"
yet there was nothing of the conspirator in their looks or
purposes, nor could even the most prejudiced doubt the
sincerity of their intentions.

Colonel Ellis, who was a natural born leader, set the
example he would have the others follow by grasping
the hand of the man nearest to him; and so hands were
grasped, till the thirty-five men present formed a living
chain about the long table in the center of the room.

After this there was less restraint, and men who had
scarcely dared to whisper their hopes or fears became
free and outspoken in giving them expression.

Among the Americans present was a handsome young
man, Arthur Loring, a graduate of West Point, who had
recently resigned from the army in order to take charge
of a large sugar plantation owned in Hawaii by his
father, a Boston merchant.

So far, Captain Loring, who, like most trained soldiers,
was not a fluent talker, remained silent. Colonel Ellis
had just been elected chairman of the Council, an act
that made him President of the Provisional Government, then and there established. when Captain Loring

rose to his feet, and, with more embarrassment of manner than he would have shown if ordered to charge a
battery, he saluted the chair, and said:

"While I am sure that nothing that has transpired in
this Council, or that may transpire at its subsequent con-
sultations, will ever be made public by.one of us till the
occasion for secrecy is past, yet we should not lose sight
of the fact that the spies of the Queen and her adherents
swarm in Honolulu, and where they do not know things
they will surmise the worst. While I cannot speak with
absolute certainty, yet I feel as sure as a man can in my
position that it is at this moment known at the palace
that we are here, and our purpose will be understood.
Alone, the Queen has neither the force nor the ability to
assert herself as she is ambitious to do; but she is not
lacking in advisers who make up for her deficiencies.
Be assured that the instant she is certain that we will
resist this new and illegal Constitution she will not
hesitate to enforce it by every means at her disposal.
Her army is barely fifty strong; but there are five
thousand native men who stand ready to do her bidding to the death, and in the arsenal in this city there
are arms for a large force of troops. If the adherents
of the Queen get possession of the arsenal—and they
may be in that position before another sun rises—every
man opposed to her will be arrested or be forced to
flight, or to seek the protection of the warships in the
harbor. Therefore, my friends, as a matter of prudence
we should organize a military force at once, seize the
arsenal and disarm all the Queen's troops. If in this
work I can be of any service, as a private in the ranks
or an officer, command me to the death."

This sensible and spirited speech was received with

applause. It suggested more than a theory. In it the
Council saw a tangible something that could be carried
into effect at once; and, while it implied force, which
even the boldest was anxious to avoid, the most timid
realized that it was only by a show of force that the
Queen could be intimidated and bloodshed averted.

With the promptness of earnest men who had a great
deal to do and a short time to do it in, the skeleton of a
military organization was at once formed, the command
of the Provisional regiment being given by acclamation
to Captain Loring, who, from that minute on, was addressed as "colonel," and so we shall give him his Hawaiian rank.

Colonel Loring was quite right when he declared that
this meeting at the hotel was known at the palace, with
the names of all who attended.

Queen Liliuokalani, like most of the sovereigns in the
world to-day, would not be considered above the mass
in intellect, if she was of the mass; but she had the
cunning that is a good substitute for mental ability, and
then the adulation paid her because of her position gave
her an exalted idea of her own abilities, and led her to
transcend her prerogatives in the direction of affairs.

With good educational advantages, the Queen is not
even fairly well educated. Brought up amid Christian
influences and surroundings, she has chosen to ignore
religion by holding aloof from it, and so giving her
enemies a basis for the rumor that she has gone back to
the bloody orgies and festishes of her forefathers. But
be that as it may, certain it is that she had come to
regard the beautiful islands of Hawaii as her own ex-
clusive property, on which foreigners could only live

by her sufferance; and this she had made up her mind not to continue.

If the Queen, like Kohala, had been moved to effort by the high resolve of elevating her people instead of aggrandizing herself, she might have ranked as a wise ruler, and even the most ardent advocate of a republic would never have dreamed of revolution while she reigned. But she began in error, and tried to justify her blunders by additional folly.

Even while Colonel Loring was talking at the Hawaiian Hotel and an army was being formed to depose her the Queen, with a few white men and many native adherents about her, was discussing, in her own private apartments, the purpose of the white men's meeting.

From time to time a native messenger came into the Queen's presence, bearing the name of the last arrival at the room of the Council in the Hawaiian Hotel.

One of the Queen's ministers was an American named Eli Porter, or, rather, he had been an American, but now he was a citizen of Hawaii. He was a man of wealth, and he was further bound to the islands and Her Majesty by his marriage with her cousin, a full-blooded native. To this man the Queen now looked for advice. News of the breaking up of the Council had just come in, and Her Majesty turned to Mr. Porter, in whose abilities and fidelity she had all faith, to surmise what had been done.

"I can tell," said Mr. Porter, with an assurance that carried conviction, "exactly what these men have done."

"Then ease my doubts by telling me without questioning," said the Queen, her dark face twitching with excitement.

"They are planning to depose Your Majesty; but to do

that with success, they must either organize an army at once or declare their fears and ask for the protection of the American warships now here. Your Majesty has only sixty armed soldiers, the palace guards, and these can soon be overpowered; but, by acting promptly, we can soon have Honolulu swarming with your defenders."

Seeing that her minister paused for her comment on this, the Queen asked:

"How can this be done?"

"There are arms for five thousand men in Your Majesty's arsenal, and there are five thousand Hawaiians ready to seize them, if you give the order."

"I do give the order!" she said, impetuously.

"Then I shall have the guards seize the arsenal at once," and, in his eagerness, Porter rose to his feet as if he were about to carry out this purpose immediately; but he stopped as if struck by another thought, and began stroking his chin.

"What detains you?" asked the Queen, impatiently.

"Another matter of equal importance, Your Majesty," said Porter.

"What is it?"

"Kohala."

"What of him?"

"The revolutionists, as Your Majesty knows, are imposing on many of your people by declaring that this young man, as a direct descendant of King Kamehameha, is the rightful heir to the throne, and Kohala helps the imposition by a strong belief in his own claims."

"He is a fool!" she said, angrily.

"No doubt; but he can become a very dangerous one to our cause. He is, as Your Majesty knows, an outspoken republican, yet he could be made to compromise

with his convictions by permitting himself to be made
president for life."

"What folly!" said Her Majesty, with a shrug of her
broad shoulders.

"Not such folly, if their plans carry."

"What plans?"

"Why, the principal plan is that Kohala shall at once
marry Leila, daughter of Keona of Hawaii. The two,
as Your Majesty may remember, were betrothed when
they were children, and, although Kohala has seen much
of the world since then, and so may have no love for the
daughter of the chief, yet his love for the people of these
islands is so strong that it is firmly believed he can be
made to do anything that promises a realization of his
rather romantic dreams. But in Kohala himself I see
no danger."

"Where, then, does it lie?"

"In his marriage with Leila. Not even Your Majesty
has more influence over the people of Hawaii than Keona.
He, as you well know, has never been your friend. If
his daughter becomes the wife of Kohala he will have
a double reason for opposing you—his personal hate and
his family pride. Your Majesty's husband was a white
man, and, as you know, the people never liked it. With
the daughter of a chief for his wife, Kohala can appeal
to the pride of the natives, and they will flock to his
support. And, let me add, the Americans, nearly all of
whom are Your Majesty's enemies, strongly favor this
marriage."

"But, Mr. Porter," said the Queen, with a compression
of the very full lips, "how would you stop it?"

"There are two ways of doing it," replied Porter.

"What are they?"

Speaking very slowly, and looking down at a paper held in his hand as if he saw the words there. Porter said:

"Sovereigns·with devoted subjects have never had much trouble in getting rid of a rival—of the rival he met at the start."

"I do not quite·understand; but let that go. What is the second way of making this young man harmless?" and the Queen half closed her eyes and looked up at the ceiling.

"I would marry him to a white woman at once."

"But what good would that do?"

"It would array Keona and all the natives against him."

"You think so?"

"I am sure of it."

"But would they come to my side?"

"They might. Again, by marrying such a woman, he would alienate the Americans."

"'Ah!" exclaimed the Queen, and she brought her fat palms together with a smack, "that is what we want. We must alienate the Americans from him; would that we could banish them from Hawaii at the same time."

CHAPTER V.

MRS. HOLMES IN A QUANDARY.

MARGUERITE HOLMES was much talked about in Honolulu. She was a woman who would attract attention wherever she went, yet it could not be said with truth

that she courted notoriety; it came to her. She impressed one at first as being shrinking, if not reserved,
still she soon became a center of attraction, particularly
to elderly men, over whom she seemed to exercise a
peculiar fascination.

Young men did not take kindly to her, though when
she chose to exercise her remarkable powers she could,
as we have seen in the case of Kohala and Captain
Featherstone, bring them to her feet.

When at home Mrs. Holmes occupied her time in writing or in arranging her own dresses; the latter never
followed the lines of fashion, but were cut and draped
with an eye to her own figure and complexion; and the
consequence was that, with the simplest materials, she
always managed to look the best and the most tastefully
dressed woman in any gathering where she was a guest.

When not a nimated in conversation Mrs. Holmes's
face seemed pinched and wan, and the long-lashed eyes
had in them a sorrowing, introverted expression that
made her look older than the years she claimed.

She was bending over her sewing to-night in a little
bow-windowed apartment that was hÃlf boudoir, half
sitting-room, when the angular and taciturn Clem
entered, and said:

"Captain Featherstone, mem."

"Show him in, Clem," said Mrs. Holmes.

On the instant the expression of age and heart-torture
vanished, and the childlike light of innocence and ex-
pectancy came into the remarkable eyes.

"I hardly expected you to-night, captain," she said,
as, without rising, she extended to him her left hand.
The right still held the needle and the sewing was on her
lap.

"Nor would I have disturbed you again, Flossy, if it were not that I am in trouble," said Featherstone.

"In trouble?" she echoed.

"Yes."

"But I hope not in danger?"

"Every suspected man and woman in Honolulu to-night is in danger; but men who play for large stakes must take some risks." Then, as if putting himself aside, he asked: "When have you seen Kohala?"

"To-day."

"He came here?"

"He did."

"And how did he seem?"

"Much worried. He told me that he must leave to-morrow for Hilo."

"For Hilo?"

"Yes. There is to be a meeting of all the native opponents of the Queen in a great cave near the lake of fire, where, for centuries, the chiefs of Hawaii have assembled whenever there was danger. The message has come to him through Keona, a powerful chief on that island. He says that, for the sake of the people whom he so loves, he dare not disobey. Ah! I fear there is going to be trouble—bloodshed!" cried Marguerite, and she interlocked her thin fingers above her sewing and looked imploringly at the captain, as if asking him to allay her fears.

"Do you fear for yourself?" asked Featherstone.

"No; I am not a coward," she said, with spirit.

"Then you fear for him?"

"Why should I not fear for him? Can any woman with a heart remain indifferent to the man who pays her the

greatest compliment it is possible for man to pay? I
would do much to help him and to save him."

. "Pardon me, Flossy. You are quite right. I am apt
to forget my true mission here in my love for you. But,
. tell me, does he still persist on an immediate marriage?"

"He does."

"And your answer?"

"I have obeyed your instructions. I will not promise
to be his wife till he becomes the king of Hawaii and
makes England an ally. This, I told him, will prove
that his love for me, while a private citizen, has not
been changed by his becoming a king."

"Ah! Flossy, you are a natural born diplomat," said
Featherstone, admiringly. He was about to continue,
when Clem rapped at the door—something she never did
when her mistress was alone—and entered before she
heard a response.

"A lady, mem," said Clem, and she handed Mrs.
Holmes a card, then withdrew to the door, which she
held ajar.

"Mercy!" exclaimed Marguerite, and the card
trembled in her hand. "It is the Queen! She must
not see you here!"

"But I cannot get out without seeing her!" cried
Featherstone, and he rose to his feet and looked about
him.

"Quick! there is a closet!" Mrs. Holmes pointed to
a door behind her, and on the instant Featherstone
vanished.

She rose, put away her sewing, glanced at her face in
the mirror, adjusted the violet blossoms at her throat
and went out to meet her visitor.

Although heavily veiled, no one familiar with the figure of the Queen could be mistaken as to her identity. She had left her carriage in a street near by and come to this cottage alone and on foot.

Bending down and kissing the little Englishwoman on the cheek, the Queen whispered:

"My dear, take me where we can talk without being disturbed. Here, your boudoir will suit," and before Mrs. Holmes, who was about to suggest the bedroom, could respond Her Majesty led the way, for this was not her first visit.

"Are you sure we can talk here without being observed?" asked the Queen, as she dropped into a large wicker chair and wiped her face.

"Ye—yes; we can talk here in safety," replied Mrs. Holmes, with the slightest tremor in her low, sweet voice.

"I am in trouble—in sore trouble," began Her Majesty. "I am surrounded by enemies, men to whom I and my ancestors have given a home and a welcome, and scarce knowing where to turn for a friend whom I can trust, I have come to you, for you, at least, are true, and you, more than any one in Honolulu, can help me."

"I am Your Majesty's to command," said Marguerite, with a self-deprecating shake of the head; "but I am so weak and helpless that I cannot see how I can be of service to any one, much less to the good Queen of Hawaii."

"You will be entirely frank with me?"

"Surely, Your Majesty."

"Do you love Kohala?" and the Queen straightened up and fastened her big black eyes on the little widow.

"I am not indifferent to Kohala," replied Marguerite.
and she looked down on her thin interlocked fingers, as
was her habit when particularly serious. "But," she
continued, "I cannot forget that I am only recently a
widow, and that I am not as yet physically strong."

"But Kohala is rich."

"That would be no inducement to me."

"And he is handsome."

"I concede that."   .

"And well educated, though I think you white people
give too much importance to mere learning. But there
is one thing a woman values more than wealth, beauty
or education."

"What is that, Your Majesty?"

"Love! The young man loves you."

"I am afraid he does."

"And by that chain of love you can lead him where
you will. Are you ready to do it to help me?"

"Your Majesty, my mind is dull to-night and my
heart is heavy; I do not understand," said Marguerite,
appealingly.

"Then I shall be plainer." The Queen drew her chair
nearer, and, sinking her voice to a whisper that seemed
masculine in its hoarseness, she continued: "If you
marry Kohala at once it can be kept secret till such time
as you choose to disclose it. I will see to it that he leaves
immediately after the ceremony, which can take place
to-morrow morning at the palace, and there you can
remain under my protection—the protection of a loving
mother—so long as you are content with such a friend
and such a home. Wait, do not stop me. I am not rich.
but I command wealth and power. Do as I ask you, and
there will be nothing in my gift to grant for which you

will need to ask a second time. Now, what say you, my
precious friend?"

"It is so—so sudden," said Mrs. Holmes, her eyes still
on the interlocked fingers.

"But I cannot wait. I must have your answer to-
night; at once!" and the Queen rose and towered above
the little widow like a gigantic silhouette.

"But I must have the night to consider," said Marguerite, with an upward glance at the full, swarthy face of
the Queen.

"This night?"

"Yes, this night."

"And your answer will be ready in the morning?"

"It will."

"And you will fetch it to the palace?"

"If Your Majesty desires it."

"I do desire it. I shall see you not later than nine
o'clock?"

"If Your Majesty so orders."

"No. I so request. I never order those whom I love."

Marguerite, following her guest's example, rose, and,
on the instant, the big, strong arms were about her little
neck, and the Queen, after kissing her on both cheeks,
withdrew.

"Well!" exclaimed Featherstone, as he emerged from
the closet, "I am glad she has gone, and I am equally
glad that I had an opportunity to hear her proposition."

"And I am sorry that you have heard it. I do not like
the idea of playing traitor," said Marguerite, the pinched,
weary expression again coming into the childish, ir-
resolute face.

"And what are you going to do?"

She raised her hands to her face, let them fall helplessly, and half sobbed:

"I do not know. I have been following your instructions. You are a man, and strong; I am a woman, and
weak. What do you advise?"

"You cannot permit an actual marriage—for my sake."

"And yet you are willing that I should pretend to an
illegal marriage so that you can hold this man to your
purpose and eventually marry me yourself; is not that
it?"

"That is exactly it. It is in our power, through Kohala
and his followers, to make Hawaii an English colony, the
property of the British crown. If we win—and I am sure
we can—it means a fortune for you and me. One hundred thousand pounds will be the reward of our success.
With such a fortune and with such a wife, I shall be the
happiest man in the world."

"But what must I do?" she asked.

"I have already told you. You must get him to issue
a proclamation, calling on the Hawaiians to sustain him
as their legal king, and to depose the Queen as a pretender. Such an act on his part will give England her
opportunity; we shall then have a majority of the natives
behind us, and the rest will be easy. Indeed, after the
deposition of the Queen and the crowning of Kohala, it
would be better for my purpose if the gilded young
savage were found dead in his bed some fine morning
—an event not at all impossible in such a community
as this. The adherents of the Queen could be hired for
such work, or, if not, it would be an easy matter to
place the taking off of the young man at their doors."

"Don't, don't talk in that way," she said, with a shudder. "The thought of blood makes me faint."

"Then I shall not refer to it again. You look weary, and need rest. Go to bed, and in the morning call on Her Majesty. Agree to anything and everything but the actual performance of the marriage ceremony with Kohala. I can see, if you do not, exactly why the Queen is so eager to have you Kohala's wife. Now, good-night and pleasant dreams, little girl."

Featherstone drew her to his side, brought her passive head to his broad breast and kissed her. But even after he withdrew she stood for some minutes as if in a trance, and the lines about her eyes and mouth were as those of an old woman.

CHAPTER VI.

THE INFERNO OF HAWAII.

IN the southeast corner of the great island of Hawaii, after which the whole group of islands is named, there is the most wonderful if not the most famous volcano in the world—Kilauea—pronounced Kil-awe-ee-ah. It is a vast lake of fire far up among the clouds, and on its scorching shores the molten waves break at times like the phosphorescent rollers over the coral reefs that encircle the island.

The sun had dropped behind great banks of flaming clouds, that looked as if they had caught in their huge folds the reflection of the mighty crater, when bands of natives could be seen coming up from Hilo and the many emerald valleys about to the blistering sconia banks that surrounded the surging lake of fire.

Although the Hawaiians ordinarily dress like the Americans of their class, on this occasion each man and woman wore the picturesque native costume. The men carried spears tipped with the serrated teeth of the shark, and their helmets were decorated with the bright plumage of paroquettes. They wore sandals with shark-hide soles, and their oval shields, ornamented with iridescent shells, were of the same tough material.

As is their custom when they meet to practice the ancient rites, which all the pleadings of the missionaries have not induced them wholly to relinquish, the women wore robes of colored grass, of the shape and woven in the patterns of the Scottish kilt. The raven hair, hanging loose down their shoulders, looked blacker in contrast with the crimson blossoms with which it was intertwined, while great wreaths of wildflowers took the place of jackets about the bronzed necks and shoulders.

As the young women advanced, they sang, as if unmindful of the steep ascent, and formed a body-guard about one who seemed to be the youngest and most beautiful, as she surely was the most honored, of the troop. This was Leila, daughter of Keona, the hereditary chief of the great island of Hawaii. Leila looked beautiful when seen in evening-dress at the last ball given by the Queen in Honolulu; but in her native attire she appeared far more radiant and captivating, nor was this costume a greater strain on her innate modesty.

The inner rim of the great crater is honeycombed with volcanic caves. Some of these, particularly near the sea of fire, are of recent origin, and are continually changing their forms, or are being destroyed and replaced by others equally weird and fantastic. Near the outer rim of the crater, at certain points, there are igneous caverns

of great extent that have not changed materially since
the days of which tradition tells, when the whole island
was for a time one vast cone of fire, whose heaven-reach-
ing torch dimmed the splendor of the cloudless sun at
high noon.

Time out of mind one of these ancient caverns, that
might have served as a chamber for Vulcan, has been
used as a council chamber by the chiefs of Hawaii.   Here
the great Kamehameha announced his purpose to his
warriors before he began the campaign that resulted
in subduing all the islands to his sway.   Here the chiefs ·
of Hawaii had been married since long before the coming of Captain Cook, and here the Chief Keona had
met his followers in council when the increasing aggres-
sions of the white men or the imbecility and vices of
their own rulers threatened the liberties of the people.

Keona of Hawaii was a man in the prime of life, tall
and finely formed, as are ever the high-class natives, and
with a bearing and physiognomy that denoted unusual
strength and activity and the heaven-given power to
command.

Keona, seated on a lava block, that looked like a
Titan's throne by the light of the many shell lamps that
illuminated the cave, was dressed in the barbaric but
becoming feather robes of gold-bronze, such as his warlike ancestors ever wore in council.   About him were
fivescore or more men, all carrying spears and shields,
and all showing by the serious expression on their
swarthy faces that business of unusual importance was
to be transacted to-night.

The chief and his followers were talking in low, earnest tones when, suddenly, like music from the sky, that
was re-echoed with thrilling effect in the depths of the

cavern, the song of the Hawaiian maidens could be
heard, and then the men became silent—

> "Fringing with crimson crest
>   Those watch-towers of the west,
> Which lift their cold, gray battlements on high.
>   The monarch of the day
>   Veils his last lingering ray,
> And sinks to rest o'er far-off Waianæ.
>
> " No sound is on the shore
>   Save reef-bound breakers' roar,
> Or distant boatsman's song, or seabird's cry;
>   And hushed the inland bay
>   In stillness, far away
> Like phantoms rise the hills of Waianæ.
>
> " Ghosts of each act and thought
>   Which the dead day has wrought,
> The misty twilight shadows silent fly
>   To burial, 'neath the pall
>   Of 'past' beyond recall,
> Which falls with night o'er silent Waianæ."

With Leila in their midst, the girls advanced through
the open ranks, and when within twenty feet of him
Keona descended and led his daughter to a seat by his
side. This appeared to be a signal, for at once the women began a song that had to it a more martial ring,
and to its stirring measure the warriors kept perfect
time by beating their spears against their resonant
shields.

The last notes of this song were still echoing down the
cavern when a series of shrill cries, that might well
have alarmed people not expecting them, came from
the profound and stygian depths beyond.

Neither the chief nor those about him seemed startled.
nor turned in the direction of the sound as it came nearer

and swelled out in shriller and more piercing notes. At length, a band of three old men and three old women, dressed in robes of rattling reeds, and with huge gray wigs of dried seaweeds on their heads, appeared before the chief and his daughter, and prostrated themselves at his feet, and so remained till he told them to rise.

These were the Kahinas, or sorcerers of the island, people with prophetic powers who could pierce the veil of the future and tell all that was to be, though their prophecies, like those of the oracles of an older and more cultured people, were invariably enigmatical, and were capable of the most opposite interpretations.

One of these Kahinas was a man who looked to be older, as he certainly was more hideous, than any of his companions. He stood closer to the chief than the others, as became the rank of the oldest priest on all the islands. Addressing him, Keona asked:

"Can Helna tell us why tarries our king?"

"We have no king, alas!" replied the old man, and he emphasized the exclamation by raising his long wand and letting the end fall to the rocky floor with a metallic ring, an example followed, like a chorus, by the other Kahinas.

"But Hawaii shall soon have a king!" said Keona.

"We shall soon have a king!" shouted the warriors, and the girls threw back their long black tresses, and chanted:

"We shall soon have a king!"

"Where is Kohala?" asked the chief.

"He is here," said Helna.

The old sorcerer raised to his lips a shell bugle, which he carried fastened to his girdle, and blew a long, shrill blast, that went echoing down through the cave as if a

thousand mystic buglers were prolonging the notes, with
an ever-decreasing force, in the far-off depths.

A brief silence, then the quick fall of hurrying feet
could be heard coming up as if from lower depths.
Nearer and nearer came the tramping, then a song of
triumph burst from the lips of unseen men. A flash
of flambeaux banished the stygian blackness behind.
Then men came to view, shaking their torches till
the place seemed filled with a rain of fire. These
people were dressed as warriors, and in their midst,
with a corona of crimson feathers on his head and a
yellow mantle that flashed like gold over his shoulders,
was Kohala, the sole descendant of the great King
Kamehameha, who, in this very chamber, had begun
his career of triumph.

When Leila saw the young man the color deepened
on her olive cheeks, and she would have risen as her
father had done had he not bent over her and whispered :

"She who is to be the Queen of Hawaii need not rise
in any presence."

At sight of the youth whom they regarded as their
rightful king the men broke into a cheer, or, rather,
a long, shrill shout, that resembled the cries of startled
eagles.

Keona descended from the seat, and, catching Kohala
to his breast, he kissed him on both cheeks, and, still
holding him in his strong embrace, he turned his face
to the people and cried out :

"I told you that one day I should show you your king.
Behold ! Kohala, from wandering through all lands, has
come back to Hawaii, the home of his heart, and he will
leave us never again.'

Again the cheering broke out, the spears were beaten against the shields and the torch-bearers shook their brands till all seemed deluged in a gólden rain.

"I am not the king of Hawaii, but I am better: I am a Hawaiian, who loves his home and his people, and who is ready, if need be, to lay down his life for both," said Kohala, in a voice that all could hear, while the warmth of his reception and the barbaric surroundings stirred in his heart the latent spirit of his ancestors, and brought the blood in darker waves to his cheeks and kindled a heroic light in the great black eyes.

The young man bowed to Leila, whom he now saw for the first time since his entrance, and the look of sudden and transitory pain that flitted over his handsome face may have passed unnoticed by others, but it did not escape the keen gaze of the old sorcerer, Helna.

Yielding to the many arms that fairly lifted him up, Kohala stood before Leila, kissed her hand with the gallantry of a medieval knight, and then, in obedience to the request—it seemed like a command—of Keona, he sat down beside the beautiful girl.

"When Kohala weds Leila, the daughter of Keona of Hawaii, then shall he be crowned and placed on the throne now disgraced by her who calls herself 'Queen' at Honolulu!'" called out Helna, who felt that he might venture on that prophecy with perfect safety.

And to the people who heard him, and who all believed the same thing before he had spoken, Helna was more than ever the most wonderful Kahina Hawaii had ever seen.

"We have met to-night," said Keona, addressing himself to Kohala and to his eager-faced followers, "not to see the wedding of a prince nor the crowning of a

king—though they will speedily follow to-night's work
—but to welcome him who is to be our ruler, and to see
him, as we now do, seated beside her to whom he was
betrothed when a boy and while yet his father lived.
I have heard wild stories about Kohala's admiration for
women whose skins are whiter than is Leila's of Hawaii;
but it troubles me not, for I knew that the son of such a
father could never break his father's word. To-night we
would learn the plans of Kohala, assuring him that with
our lives we stand ready to carry them out."

CHAPTER VII.

LOVE OR PATRIOTISM—WHICH?

THE men and the maidens and the weird Kahinas
gathered about the volcanic throne on which Kohala
and Leila were seated thought, nor took pains to hide
their thoughts, that they had never seen two such beautiful young people before.

The bronzed cheeks of Keona were aglow, and the
fire of pride and triumph burned in his keen black eyes,
for the act on which all his hopes centered since the
birth of his daughter was soon to be consummated. Nor
was it paternal ambition alone that moved him. At
heart, he was a patriot. Too circumscribed in his en-
vironment to look upon all men as his brothers, all the
love of his strong nature was concentrated on his own
people; and, to make them free and independent, he
would have seen with delight the last white man dead
or banished from Hawaii.

"Friends and a feast await us by the shore!" called

out the old priest, Helna. "Let our king make his
pledge before all the chiefs ere we leave this the sacred
temple of Hawaii."

At a signal from the old Kahina, Kohala rose, and
Leila, in obedience to her father's gesture, did the same.

"Kohala, son of the conqueror," said Helna, in a low,
solemn voice, while Keona and all the people crossed
their hands on their breasts and bowed their heads, "are
you ready to keep the vows your father made to all our
people in your behalf?"

The young man hesitated, and swallowed an invisible
lump. He cast a quick, nervous glance at the beautiful
girl by his side, then said, with an effort and in a voice
that seemed strange to himself:

"I am."

"Then you have not been changed by living in the
land of the whites?" said Helna.

"My love for Hawaii and for the people of my race
has grown stronger," said Kohala, with more confidence.
"Yet am I changed from a simple-minded boy to a man
who has learned the secret of the white man's power,
and who is ready to use that knowledge for the good of
his own people."

A murmur of approval went up from the groups about
the great volcanic rock on which Kohala stood, and the
men raised their faces.

"Our people look to you to bring them light in this
the day of their great doubt and darkness; are you
ready?"

"I am."

"And you will marry Leila, the pearl of Hawaii, and
wrest from the impostor the throne of your fathers?"
said Helna.

It was well for Kohala that this was a double question. His was not a nature to be indifferent to the rare advantages of the beautiful girl by his side. He knew and felt that in every physical grace she was not only the peer, but vastly the superior of the white woman who had gained such an irresistible mastery over his heart; yet the full knowledge of this fact intensified rather than weakened his love for Marguerite Holmes.

Hawaii, with the woman of his heart, would be heaven; without her, any and every condition would be torture. He realized his own helplessness. He felt that his love was a chain bearing him down and weakening his manhood at the very time when he needed more strength; yet he would not have forgotten his idol if he could, nor have been free from her magic spell if in his power.

Keeping in mind the last of the old Kahina's questions, Kohala replied:

"I believe in rulers chosen by the people who are to be ruled; but my life among the whites has given me a contempt for kings who claim that the gods have chosen them for such a mission. The Queen of Hawaii is not the choice of our people. She regards the throne as her private property, so that if she were, as I am, the descendant of the great King Kamehameha, still should I oppose her, still should I demand that she do right by yielding what she was wrong in accepting. So sure am I that the people should elect their own rulers that I will not insist on my claims that are just as a birthright. The people of Hawaii, the people of our race, who are the rightful owners of the land, must by their votes say who it is they want to have rule over them, and if it be another than myself I will show my faith in my own counsel by yielding the earliest and most continued obedience."

Keona and his daughter, of all the people present, were the only ones who fully comprehended Kohala's reply, and it was evident from the expression of the chief that he did not indorse the views of the regal young republican. He was still moved by the old traditions as to rank; he was himself a chief by right of birth, and a greater right than that was beyond his comprehension. Yet he had the wisdom to see that where the people might be divided as to the choice of a ruler, as they certainly were in Hawaii, that it would add to the security of Kohala's throne if a majority of the people indicated him as their choice.

"It shall be even as Kohala says," called out the chief. "With the morrow's sun I will dispatch young men who can read and write to all the islands, and they shall find who is the choice of the people. This we shall do to please Kohala, for there can be no doubt as to the result. But when he is our king—and he surely will be —he will hold us the stronger to him the more he ignores the laws and customs of the whites. Our motto must be: 'A king of our own, and Hawaii for the Hawaiians!'"

This was said with a fire and an energy that were contagious, and when the chief turned to the faces of the people about him he saw a new light in the eyes of the men, who gave expression to their approval in a cheer that echoed down the cavern depths for fully a minute after.

"Kohala will give his heart to the wishes of his people; that we know, and that the people believe, and so will they give him their faith, and, if need be, their lives.

We shall know all when the next full moon rises over
Hawaii; then we shall meet here to greet the king and
his queen, and our boats will be ready to take them, as
befits their rank, to the palace at Honolulu. Now let
us descend to the shore where other friends await us
with a feast."

So spoke Helna, who, in addition to his priestly duties,
acted as master of ceremonies to the great chief Keona,
to whom he was warmly attached.

Fresh torches were lit, and the Kahinas took the advance; then came the girls, with Leila in their midst,
while the men with spears formed in advance of and to
the rear of the chief and Kohala; and so the procession
went down to the shore, but not as the people had come.

By a descent, sometimes steep, and again as smooth
and hard and glistening as a floor of polished steel, the
Kahinas led the way through the rocky cavern. The
torches flashed on black side chambers, like cells set
in the walls of a mighty prison, or they turned to blood
the subterranean streams that crossed or ran along their
course.

The way was familiar to every person but Kohala,
who had not visited the cavern since he was a child of
seven, and then it was to be betrothed to the infant
daughter of the chief.

It was well that etiquette required the young man to
keep silent as he went down through the sacred, black
depths, for his heart was anxious and full, but not with
the cares of Hawaii.

At length from the far front there came the dull
booming, as of distant guns, accompanied by a ceaseless
roar that might have shook steadier nerves than those
of the Hawaiians had they not known. that the booming

was caused by the fall of the breakers on the barrier reef and the roar by the ceaseless flow and recession of the waves on the shell-lined shore.

The exit from the cave was guarded by a regiment of plume-crowned palms, over which the moon, now at its full, poured a peaceful, silvery light that added to the calm grandeur of the scene.

As soon as the procession came into the light the men to the rear sent up a long, shrill shout, that was answered by another and a more prolonged shout by men in the direction of the shore, along which a number of fires, like blazing fountains, sent plumes of flame into the sky.

Then the companions of Leila began to sing:

" Hail to the king and his bride,
    Men of the hills and the sea,   .
    Kohala has come from the white land
    To the green vales of fair Hawaii."

Fully two thousand men and women were gathered about the fires on the shore, and the swarms of outrigger canoes drawn up on the beach told how a majority of the people must have come.

They had prepared a great feast in honor of the king, for such they now regarded Kohala. Meats and fish, vegetables and fruit, and the national dish, "poi," all crowned with flowers, as were the lithe maidens who served the banquet, found sharp appetites to appreciate them; but the honored guest—and, it may be, Leila— were the only persons present who did not enjoy the feast.

Finely woven mats, spread on the ground and bordered by flowers, served as tables; and tea was handed round

in fancifully carved cocoanut-shells.   It was a native
banquet, plus many things unknown till the coming
of the whites.   .

The eating was accompanied with songs and shouts of
laughter, and many of the jests directed by the girls at
Leila were so personal, though invariably pleasant, that
the beautiful girl was kept in a state of blushing agitation.

As soon as the feast was over the older men lit their
pipes and drew back some distance so as to leave a wide,
open space between them and the fires.   Back of these
the young men stood up with their shields on their left
arms and their right hands grasping their spears about
the center.

Kohala and Keona, with Leila between them, sat on
a raised seat that looked like a bank of gorgeous flowers,
and back of them were brilliant groups of women, all
blossom-crowned and all showing by their display of
white teeth and flashing black eyes their intense enjoyment of the occasion.

In Hawaii, as in all the Pacific Islands to the south,
dancing is a part of every religious and festal gathering.
It is said that Samra and New Zealand were colonized
by the Hawaiians.   The language, folk-lore and customs
common to all would indicate a common ancestry; but,
be that as it may, the dancing of the "hoola" girls, as
the young women skilled in the graceful art are called,
is as popular in Hawaii to-day as it was when the natives
welcomed and entertained Captain Cook more than a
century ago.

As soon as the space was cleared before the great cen-
tral fire a band of twoscore girls, crowned and draped
with flowers till they resembled animated bouquets,

sprang with airy grace into the opening, saluted Kohala and the chief, and then, at a signal given by the clapping of the leader's hands, the wonderful dance began.

The music was supplied by the singing of a group of women seated on the ground, and the changes in the graceful mazes were made to the rhythmic beating of the spears on the shields.

In addition to being an exquisite dance, such as would have made the fame and fortune of the *maitre de ballet* who could have produced it on the stage, this was also a most expressive pantomime. The ardor of the lover and the coyness of the maiden were pictured with an excellence and delicacy that amounted to art. The jealousy of rivals, the opposition of friends, the secret meetings, the agony of parting, and then the elopement, the capture, the reconciliation and the marriage, were all depicted in a way that could not have been made more poetic and dramatic by the use of words.

Leila gradually lost her self-consciousness and became enraptured with the scene. The pearly teeth flashed through the parted carnation of her lips. Her long-lashed black eyes were aglow, and, forgetting herself in the excitement of the occasion, she added her voice to those of the singing women at her feet.

Now and then she shot a glance at the face of the young man seated by her side, and she wondered that he could be so cold and impassive amid such a glow of joyous excitement. How could she know that his thoughts were with his heart in the cottage of the white woman at Honolulu?

CHAPTER VIII.

OPENING THE EYES OF LOVE.

COLONEL ELLIS had been a resident of Hawaii since the
close of the great war in his own land.   His forethought
and energy had made him rich; but while this was the
purpose of his voluntary exile, he regarded as his own
the rights of the natives of Hawaii.

The indifference of the Queen to the moral standards
that prevail in cultured communities, her weakness in
yielding to the influence of selfish favorites and her fierce
defiance of the constitutional restraints that environed
the throne were seen and their consequences appreciated by Colonel Ellis before others, who were equally
involved in the consequences, dreamed of their danger.

It was Colonel Ellis who induced Kohala to spend six
years at school in America and Europe.   It was Colonel
Ellis who cared for the young man's estates and made
them as productive and profitable as his own; and it was
the colonel who early instilled into the mind of the youth
those principles of republicanism that gave him such a
contempt for hereditary rulers.

Colonel Ellis and the men associated with him had
fully resolved to check the mad course of the Queen by
making vacant the throne; but they had the wisdom to
see that a native figure of some kind must be kept on or
near that ornamental seat, so as to appease the feelings
of the Hawaiians.

With Kohala in power, Colonel Ellis saw that Hawaii

would be practically republican, and that he could, through the influence of this young man, bring the natives to his way of thinking, and in time make real his dream of annexation to the land from which he had himself been so long an exile.

It had been decided by the Americans that if the marriage of Kohala could be made to play a part in the drama now on the stage at Honolulu it would be good diplomacy and sound statesmanship to have him marry the Princess Kaiulani, then at school in England, and whom Queen Liliuokalani had selected to succeed herself on the throne.

There appeared to be one thing on which all the friends and foes of Kohala were agreed, and that was that he would serve their purpose better by marrying some one at once.

As we have seen, the natives who opposed the Queen and who were led by Keona, regarded his marriage with Leila, the daughter of the chief of Hawaii, as practically settled. Many of the Americans were anxious, for reasons of State policy, that he should marry the half-bred schoolgirl Kaiulani, who must come at once from England for that purpose, though they would not seriously object to Leila.

The Queen was resolved that Kohala should marry the Englishwoman, Marguerite Holmes, for she well knew that such a course would mean his own political suicide, and hers was the one scheme that entirely met the young man's approval.

The English were not so much interested in the young man's marriage as that he should be induced to raise the banner of revolt and declare himself king, when their Government could step in as a peacemaker between the rivals, and, seizing the islands till the quarrel could be adjusted, see to it that it never was adjusted and the hold never released.

Among all these diverse factions the English, though working quietly and out of sight, stood the best chance of success, for they had enlisted on their side Marguerite Holmes, the one person to whose will and wishes Kohala, since their first meeting, had ever yielded implicit obedience.

Colonel Ellis was not the man to win a point at the expense of a good woman's character; but, like all manly, honest men, he loathed, above all things, that unsexed creature—the woman adventurer. He believed, from the moment he first heard of her, that Marguerite Holmes was of this character, and he resolved to expose her; but in a spirit of fairness he made up his mind, first, to learn for himself what manner of woman she was, and if she were purchasable, as he believed, to make it worth her while to leave the islands quietly and without telling Kohala. If she should refuse to do this, he and his friends must be in a position to open Kohala's eyes so that not even his unreasoning love could blind him to the character of the woman for whose uncertain and wavering affections he had been so ready to barter away his own splendid future and the happiness and prosperity of the Hawaiians whom he so loved.

To carry out his purpose Colonel Ellis secured an introduction to Mrs. Holmes, through his friend, Dr. Wallace, who was well known as one of the little widow's most ardent admirers.

Marguerite Holmes had heard of Colonel Ellis. She knew he was a widower, and the richest man on the islands; but the fact that he was a man would have been to her sufficient reason for treating him with all consideration, and bringing him under the control of her witchery.

After his introduction, Colonel Ellis asked for leave to call on Mrs. Holmes, and she graciously consented. He was a man of the world, and, withal, a knightly admirer of the sex, and so he saw that to win he must appear to come under her influence, as others had done, yet he was not the man to permit himself to be seriously influenced by a designing woman, such as he believed Mrs. Holmes to be.

He called the day after his introduction, and found Mrs. Holmes dressed in dainty fashion for the street, when she always looked her best. She was delighted to meet him again, and the expression in the long-lashed eyes and the musical voice confirmed her words.

She sat facing him in the little flower-decorated boudoir, and would have discussed the weather and other trite matters in her graceful fashion had not the colonel, with an effort that was evident, come at once to the purpose of his visit.

"Mrs. Holmes," he began, "we are threatened with troublesome times in Hawaii, and you can help to bring them about, or you can do much to prevent them."

"I?" she exclaimed, and she laid her index finger on the rim of her becoming violet bonnet. "Surely you are mistaken, Colonel Ellis. What influence for weal or woe can a poor little nobody like myself have on the affairs of Hawaii?"

"A great deal, Mrs. Holmes," was the serious response.

"But in what way?" she asked, with increasing surprise.

"You will not think me rude if I am entirely frank?"

"I cannot imagine Colonel Ellis being rude."

"Thanks. I certainly do not mean to be. But first, a question or two, which you need not answer if you have anything to conceal."

"A thousand questions, if you will."

"You are an Englishwoman?"

"I am."

"Alone in Honolulu?"

"Yes."

"And you know the man they call Captain Featherstone?"

"I have that honor," she said, more coldly.

"If you are his friend it may be well for you to know that this Captain Featherstone's conduct is not unknown to the men who have the interests of these islands at heart, and that if he persists in his present course he may have to make a sudden and unexpected exit."

"Had you not better communicate this to Captain Featherstone himself?" she asked, with a perceptible tremor of the lips.

"No; when we come to speak to this man we shall be ready to act, and we shall act in no mild way. He is your countryman, and from his visits to you we must believe that he is, at least, your friend, and so the warning must come through you; for, to be candid with you, you are regarded with suspicion," said Colonel Ellis, with the manner of a man anxious to get at the heart of the matter at once.

Marguerite Holmes's face was usually palid; now it grew ashy, and a startled look came into her eyes, yet she managed to retain her composure, as she asked:

"What have I done to excite suspicion?"

"At such times as these everything and every one is apt to excite the suspicion of the anxious. Another question: Do you know the young Hawaiian, Kohala?"

"I do," she replied.

"Very well?"

"I think I can say: Yes, very well."

"And you are his friend?"

"I mean to be."

"And he is your admirer?"

"He has, unfortunately, that bad taste," she said; then, sitting more erect and looking down at her interlocked fingers, incased in dark kid g'oves, she added: "But my friends and my likes and dislikes should be my own private affair."

"Ordinarily I should say you were quite right, but it so happens that your friends are people of public prominence in Hawaii, and there is a suspicion—whether well-founded or not I will not pretend to say—that you and this Captain Featherstone are trying to influence Kohala for your own ends. Permit me to say, as one who would come to your rescue if you needed an unselfish friend, that in trying to influence Kohala to become a tool of England's diplomacy you are working for his ruin."

"I working for the ruin of Kohala!" she exclaimed.

"Yes, quite as much as if you were planning his murder," responded Colonel Ellis.

"May I ask in what way?"

"By leading him to believe that you love him and will marry him."

"And pray why should I not love him and marry him if we are both agreed?" she asked, with spirit.

"Ordinarily there could be no opposition to such a

course; but, unfortunately for you, Kohala at this time does not belong to himself, and, unfortunately for him, you are virtually engaged to this adventurer who calls himself Captain Featherstone. I mean no offense. What I say I can prove. For our own protection we Ameri-cans have been compelled to search out the antecedents of all who are opposed to us in Hawaii; and I may say that we understand the purpose of yourself and the man with whom you are so unfortunately associated."

Colonel Ellis did not look at her while he was speaking; but as soon as he had concluded he turned his keen gray eyes to her face and saw that she was much excited, though she made a brave effort to appear calm. At length she met his gaze, and said:

"And it is to tell me this that you have come?"

"To tell you this, and much more, for I must not per-mit gallantry to stand between me and what I believe to be my duty. You can marry Captain Featherstone whenever you please, and no man in Hawaii will dare to question your right; but when you essay to make a tool of Kohala, in whom we all are interested, then for the common safety and the common good we deem it a duty to warn you. I tell you now, this must stop. If you desire to leave Honolulu I will secure you passage on the steamer that leaves here for Australia to-morrow, and I and my friends will see to it that you have means enough to keep traveling the world for years, if you so desire."

The colonel looked at her questioningly. She had now regained her well-bred self-control.

"I do not fear your covert threats," she said, very deliberately. "I am an Englishwoman, and the British

Consul at this port will see that I am guaranteed my rights."

"Go to the British Consul and mention my name. He will assure you that I have no purpose to interfere with the rights of any human being; and he will also tell you that, when in a strange land, his country's flag is powerless to protect you in violating the laws of that land."

"How am I violating the laws?" she asked.

"You are conspiring to overthrow the existing Government, and to bring Hawaii under British control. You are coquetting with a man who may be our ruler to-morrow; but I have proof that as soon as your purpose is accomplished you will leave these islands with Featherstone. There are no walls in the world that have so many ears as those of Honolulu. Now make your choice: go on with your scheme and prepare for the consequences, or quietly take your departure, and thank Heaven you are well out of a bad scrape. I shall not ask you for an answer now, but will call at this time to-morrow. I am sorry to have troubled you, but I felt it was my duty to say what I have said. Others, to whom you are quite free to report this interview, will tell you that I usually mean what I say, and I was never more in earnest in my life . Good-morning, madam."

The colonel turned and left the room, Mrs. Holmes recognizing his departure by the slightest inclination of her dainty head.

For some time after her guest had left she sat in the same chair, her long-lashed eyes fastened on her interlocked fingers and a look of unusual seriousness on her face, which had aged perceptibly during the meeting. .

Her vanity was hurt, for Colonel Ellis was the first man she had met in Honolulu who had not treated her with smiling gallantry and induced her to believe that he was impressed by her. But she had to confess to herself that she respected him all the more for his strength and candor.

After fully half an hour, during which time the taciturn Clem popped in her head to look at her, Marguerite Holmes remained absorbed in contemplation. At length she stood up, removed her bonnet and wrap, then went to her own room, and, throwing herself face downward on the bed, sobbed as if her heart were breaking.

Did she lament the attack made on Captain Featherstone? Was her heart cut at the prospect of being forced to surrender her hold on the ardent and romantic Kohala? Was her conscience stirred to life by the memory of a life error? ·Did she fret over Colonel Ellis's discovery and the prospect of her own threatened ambitions; or did she, womanlike, give way to her tears as the only comforting outlet to her own consciousness of helplessness and weakness? To these inquiries we cannot make answer, but the details of these records may enable the reader to determine.

CHAPTER IX.

KOHALA'S JEALOUSY AROUSED.

At the council called by Keona of Hawaii there was not a person present with a drop of white blood in his veins. At the feast all were natives. Such meetings were always held in secret, and guards were kept out to prevent the approach of a white man or to give warning of the same.

Formerly Americans and Englishmen, with the brutal arrogance of race superiority, have tried to force their way into such native gatherings; but the fact that such intruders were always "found missing" soon afterward and were never seen or heard of again led to the belief that the natives, though ordinarily very amiable people, were ready to defend some of their rights with their lives, and that they were quite as ready, if the occasion warranted it, to take life, as in the days of Captain Cook. There were signs in the upper sky of coming day when Keona, preceded by four tall natives bearing paddles, walked down between Kohala and Leila to the shore. The young women preceded them, singing as if the night had brought no fatigue, and the men with the spears and shields brought up the rear.

As became his rank, the canoe of Keona was the largest. Into this the chief, his prospective son-in-law and his daughter got, and then a score of strong men pushed it out from the shell-strewn sand to the smooth expanse between the barrier reef and the shore.

As soon as the canoe was afloat the four rowers sprang from the water and took their seats, without causing a roll in the light, graceful, craft.

Kohala had a misty memory of having seen such sights when a child, and particularly on the occasion of his former visit to the sacred cavern; but this did not impair the striking and picturesque novelty of his surroundings.

From his flower-covered seat beside Leila he looked about him and saw an army, or rather a flotilla, of canoes dashing from the shore, as if endowed with life, and he beheld them forming with all the regularity of trained troops on parade.

From the center of the flotilla, after all were in readiness and the fires on shore extinguished, the shell bugle of the old priest, Helna, sounded the signal to advance. This was answered by a cheer from the men; then, to the singing of the women, the rise and fall and splash of the paddles kept perfect time, and, as if directed by one power, the canoes moved up the shore.

The morning and evening twilights are brief on the lines of and within the tropics; but in Hawaii the mountains, like Mauna Loa, towering above the white shore and emerald valleys for fourteen thousand feet, catch the light of the coming sun long before he is visible to the lower world; and so, like great reflectors, they diffuse the rays and fill their surroundings with such a lovely, poetic twilight as no other land in the world enjoys. Day does not seem to come with the sun, but rather to float down, cool, calm and refreshing, from the snowy heights of the inland peaks.

Kohala, to the fine imagination peculiar to his race, added the taste and culture of the world's best schools. He had the childlike freshness and capacity for enjoyment of the savage plus the culture that comes from an eager study of all that the foremost people have done in the world's advance.

He saw the opal light turning the mountains into great beacons and flooding the shore and sea. He saw the east glowing like an amethyst, then changing to translucent ruby. He saw the pink glow on the shore and the dark emerald of the stately palms gradually growing more distinct, as if they were marching out in stately ranks to meet the canoes. He saw the black water

changing to liquid malachite and the breakers on the
barrier reef turning to banks of iridescent pearl.

The light grew more intense, and he saw the bright
eyes and eager faces of his warlike followers, and he
heard the singing of the maidens, as sweet and fresh as
when their voices first thrilled him in the sacred cavern.
The light grew brighter; the east was ablaze; the rim
of the mighty sun rose over the sea and marked out a
path that flashed, straight as an arrow and red as the
fresh heart-blood, to the shore. And the red rays turned
redder the stern brow of Keona; but they made more
beautiful, because they revealed more distinctly, the
face of Leila, who sat with bowed head by his side.

If ever a scene were calculated to absorb wholly a
man's thought it was this one. But while nothing
escaped the notice of the youth, in whose honor all this
was being done, there was one thing needed to complete
his happiness. If Marguerite Holmes were by his side
to enjoy with him, then, indeed, would the cup of his
rapture be full. But, whether down on the glowing,
pulsating sea, or up on the calm, frozen heights of
Mauna Loa, either would have been Eden with her by
his side.

The sun was half an hour high when the canoe of the
chief turned into a palm-bordered cove, the canoes of
his immediate retainers following. Before the flotilla
broke up the men rose in their canoes, raised their
paddles like poised lances, and, taking the signal from
the shell trumpets of the Kahinas, they sent up a cheer;
then the singing women rose, and, throwing toward him
the flowers that had adorned their shining black tresses,
shouted: "Long live Kohala, our king! Long live Leila,
his bride!"

Although a Hawaiian in every fiber of his being, Keona was far too great and shrewd a man to ignore the agencies whereby the white man gathered to himself wealth and power. He might be called well educated. He was a prosperous sugar planter, and he had pasture lands covered by vast herds up the mountain-sides.

His home, set amid groves of orange and lemon, and walled in by irregular ranks of cocoanut and date palm trees, was quite as grand in its way as the palace at Honolulu. His house was furnished after the American style, and an array of trained servants were ready to do his bidding; yet it was well known that, when he did not have white visitors, he dressed and ate as his ancestors had done before they knew that there was a white man in the world.

The canoes made a landing at a little pier near Keona's house; but, instead of leaving the shore, the men and women divided, one party going up the stream to a line of bathhouses, and within a few minutes all were enjoying a morning bath.

After the bath Keona escorted his guest to the house, where they found Leila and breakfast awaiting them. Kohala ate some fruit and then was escorted to a cool chamber. He lay down, and the scenes through which he had passed the night before and his last meeting with Marguerite Holmes chased each other in wild confusion through his brain, till he dropped off to sleep.

When he awoke it was high noon, and a native boy was beside the bed fanning him. In response to Kohala's question, the boy, after bowing, said, in the native tongue:

"It is the hour when the sun is the hottest and the shadows the shortest."

"And your master?

"He has ridden into the hills to look after the herds."

"And your mistress, Leila?"

"Leila bade me say, when you awoke, that she awaits you with luncheon in the arbor that overlooks the sea," said the boy, with a graceful wave of the fan in the direction from which came the sound of the breakers on the barrier reef.

Kohala rose and dressed, in European attire, which he was very glad to resume; then, guided by the lad, he went down to the beautiful, blossom-covered arbor, where he found Leila, dressed in a loose, cool white wrapper and reading a book, just as he had seen American girls doing in the shaded grounds of the best summer villas at Newport.

With an ease and grace that he had never seen surpassed, Leila bade him good-morning, gave him her soft, shapely hand and asked him how he had rested.

She was a beautiful savage in her costume of the night before; now she was a well-bred lady, without any suggestion of ornament about her person, unless it might be the single crimson blossom at her throat.

As she moved about, the loose white robe, that in itself was far from graceful, served to bring out the beauty of her lithe form and the exquisite grace of her bearing.

He would, indeed, have been a poor physiognomist who could not have told from the girl's suppressed manner and the timid glances of the soft black eyes, as she arranged the luncheon and fixed seats for herself and Kohala, that she loved him with all the fire and force of her intense nature.

As Kohala watched her he had to confess to himself that she was far more beautiful than Marguerite Holmes, and also that she was quite the Englishwoman's peer in grace and culture. He also realized that, for his own good and the good of Hawaii, it was his duty to marry this exquisite native girl. But love is as selfish as it is unreasoning.

After they had nibbléd at the fruits and drank each a glass of iced orange sherbet, Kohala said:

"It seems as if all the peace of heaven were here. Leila, as the mistress of such a home, you should be very happy."

"No man or woman can be happy," replied Leila, with her eyes fixed on the limitless sea, "so long as the heart yearns for something it does not possess."

"Surely you are not in that state?" He regretted having said this the instant he had spoken.

Although cultured and refined, the chief's daughter had not been brought up to conceal her feelings. Up to the coming of Kohala from beyond the sea she had never had a wish ungratified.

Since her earliest memory she had been taught that she was the betrothed of the youth who was yet to be the king of Hawaii. She loved to think of him in solitude, and as she grew to womanhood and he sent her his pictures from the land of the white man she tried to give life to the shadow and to picture him all she found him when he came.

It was not with her a case of love at first sight; she had loved him through all the years of her reasoning life, loved him with increasing intensity as the years rolled on, and this love culminated in the most ardent passion when she met him after his return.

She had heard of his infatuation for Marguerite Holmes, and she had seen him lavishing on the little Englishwoman the attentions for which her own heart

hungered; and she tried to allay her jealousy and to
soothe her anguish with the belief that he would change
as soon as he was freed from the allurements and temp-
tations of Honolulu, and, above all, from the influence
of the Queen, whose purpose, with keen feminine per-
ception, she saw.

Before replying to Kohala's question she looked at
him for some seconds, until he began to feel uncom-
fortable under her gaze, then said:

"Yes. I am in that state. Kohala, can you remember when we were in the cavern before last night?"

"It is to me like a dream," he replied.

"But you know why you went there?"

"Yes; I was taken there by my father."

"As I was by mine. I was then but four years of age.
You were four years older; still, from then till now in
not one hour of my waking life have the obligations of
that time been absent from my mind. While you were
in foreign lands I was praying for your return and
planning for the happier days of Hawaii that must
surely come to our race when you were their ruler
and I was your wife. Have you, too, thought of these
things, Kohala?"

"I have," he replied, with averted face.

"And you have hoped for them?"

"The happiness of my race has been the one motive
of my life. It is that that made me a student in the
white man's schools and brought me back to my native
land. But I have had no time to give to love, and I
have come to think that, no matter what our parents
may have done in the long ago, when we reached years
of discretion we should be controlled by our own hearts."

"And that is what I believe, and that is what I feel.

Think you I could not have had lovers among the best
of our own people and the richest of the whites?" she
asked, as she sat more erect, and a strange, dangerous
light came into her great black eyes.

"I am sure of it," replied Kohala, "for you are very
beautiful—more beautiful than any white woman I have
ever met, and wise as their wisest."

"But think you that I have?"

' No."

"And why have I not?"

"Because the best was not worthy of you," he said,
evasively.

"No!" she responded, with startling emphasis. "It
is because through all my life I have loved and waited
for the coming of my king! You came, and I felt that
the day that was to make me your queen was at hand.
You came. but with you came a white woman, and they
tell me that she, like a thief who cannot value what she
has stolen, has robbed me of the heart of Kohala! Is
this true?"

' Kohala's cheeks had been olive, but now they turned
red. In his confusion he rose to his feet and got so far
in his denial as to say, "No!" when a step was heard on
the shell walk near by, and the next instant Colonel Ellis
stood at the entrance of the arbor.

The colonel was well known to Leila, and, after salut-
ing the young people and telling them that he had just
come from Honolulu. he took a letter from his breast-
pocket and handed it to Kohala, saying:

"That is of great importance to you. Read it. Leila
will pardon you."

The colonel sat down and began to fan himself with
his straw hat, while Kohala stepped outside the arbor.

The young man tore off the envelope and was surprised to see that the writing was the colonel's. He read the following:

"DEAR KOHALA—You must return to Honolulu with me at once. What your friends have feared is true. The Englishwoman has deceived you. She has other lovers, and one of them she is going to marry as soon as her purpose with you is gained. This I am ready to prove to your entire satisfaction.

"Your friend, so long as you are the friend of Hawaii,
"NORMAN ELLIS."

As Kohala read he leaned against the arbor, and his lips drew back like a scabbard from his white teeth.

CHAPTER X.

BACK TO HONOLULU.

KOHALA, as if unwilling to credit the evidence of his sight, read over and over again the note Colonel Ellis had given him; then, satisfied that he had read it aright the first time, he crushed it in his right palm and stared down at the breakers on the reef without seeing them.

At length he became aware of the hum of voices in the arbor, and he came back to a comprehension of the situation.

He realized that it would not do to show Leila that he was awfully excited, lest he might be asked to explain the cause; so, with an effort of will, he brought his lips together and covered the daggerlike flash of his teeth. From his handsome face he succeeded in banishing the

fierce expression that had transformed him for the instant into an angered and unreasoning savage. But,
determined though he was, and successful though he
was in banishing from his eyes and mouth the signs of
intense hate, he was powerless to still the wild leaping
of his heart. He heard the colonel saying:

"Yes, Leila, it is all-important that Kohala should return with me at once to Honolulu. I shall leave a letter
for your father explaining why I have not remained to
see him."

"But if there is danger to Kohala in Honolulu," said
Leila, "I shall go there with you."

"But there is not, I assure you. We have enlisted a
regiment of men who are under the command of Colonel
Loring—you know him; he is betrothed to my daughter
Alice—and if any danger threatens Kohala he and his
men are ready to avert it. The Queen is using her
every effort to retain the throne; but it is rocking be-
neath her, and she must soon descend of her own volition or be hurled to the ground by the motion," said
the colonel.

"And is there danger of war?" asked Leila.

"No, I hope not; yet we realize that the best way to
avert it is to be prepared for it. But as for Kohala, fear
not for him," said the colonel, with a little laugh that
found no response in her heart. "I shall return him to
you in safety."

The colonel went to the entrance of the arbor, and was
about to call the youth for whom he had come when he
came in himself.

"Well, Kohala, what think you of that note?" asked
the colonel.

"I cannot believe it true," was the reply.

"Nor did I think you would. But your own eyes and ears will prove to you that it is every syllable true. Are you ready to leave for Hilo?"

"I am; but I must first see Keona and express to him my great gratitude for his kindness."

"I shall do that service for you," said Leila, "though my father wants no thanks for what is to him at once a duty and a pleasure. If our friend, Colonel Ellis, thinks your presence needed at once at Honolulu, go with him, for in times like these we cannot give thought to personal ease nor to ordinary courtesy, if they detain us."

"Spoken like the daughter of a chief!" cried the colonel, who had a great admiration for the beautiful girl and who was more than eager that his ward should regard her in the same light.

The colonel had come over from Hilo in a buggy drawn by a pair of his own team, and he was famed for having the fastest and best-bred horses in Hawaii.

Kohala's trunk was fastened to the shelf behind the buggy, and the horses were hitched and prancing with impatience to be off.

The young man gave Leila his hand, and he was about to raise hers gallantly to his lips when, to his surprise and confusion, she threw her graceful arms about his neck and kissed him again and again, saying, as she released him:

"My king! You are mine! You belong to Leila and Hawaii."

"Splendid girl, that Leila," said Colonel Ellis, as the horses dashed over the circular road along the coast to Hilo. "She is worth a million such creatures as that little, thin adventuress you are breaking your heart over."

"She is all you say," replied Kohala, yet internally revolting against what the colonel had said.

The young man had heard before that Marguerite Holmes had deceived others and would deceive him, yet so long as he had not the direct evidence of this fact he was unwilling to believe that she was not all she claimed to be to him.

He honored and respected Colonel Ellis, who, since his childhood, had been to him as a father, and, while he believed him noble, he tried to comfort himself with the thought that he was not true to himself in his condemnation of Marguerite Holmes.

A few minutes of silence followed this, during which time the colonel, who was smoking a cigar, succeeded in getting the spirited team down to a settled pace, which it could keep up without harm as far as Hilo, fifteen miles away.

The woman he was flying to—not the beautiful girl he had left—filled and troubled the heart of the young man.

He reasoned that other women had been false; he had read and heard of such; but what lover ever thought it possible that the woman he loved could be placed in such a category? Certainly not the youth who was undergoing his first delightful but torturing experience of the tender passion.

Coughing, to steady his nerves rather than to clear his throat, Kohala, unable longer to keep back the anguish and curiosity that filled his heart, asked:

"How did you learn, colonel, that Mrs. Holmes was deceiving me?"

"Through the best of sources," said the colonel.

"But what are they?"

"My own ears."

"But you do not know her."

"But I do."

"I was not aware of that."

"Still it is true."

"Then you must have become acquainted with her since I left."

"That is true."

"How did you come to meet her?"

"Through Dr. Wallace."

"I do not know him."

"Well, I know him. He is a fine old fellow and a widower, and, I may add, he is one of this woman's dupes. He, too, is in love with her, and believes she will accept him at the right time; and I am inclined to think she will if she does not hook a man more to her liking before she leaves Honolulu. Why, the woman had hardly set eyes on me before she began to spread her net to entrap me. But I know the tricks of the class," and the colonel blew out a cloud of smoke and laughed till the horses threatened to run away.

Speaking very slowly and as if with an effort, Kohala asked:

"Is it because of her attempt to flirt with you that you judge her?"

"Indeed it is not," said the colonel.

"Did you speak of me?"

"Yes. I brought your name up."

"But why?"

"Because I want to save you."

"And you told her so?"

"I did."

"And that is all you know against her?"

"No, Kohala, for her own sake I wish it were."

"Do you object to telling me the reason for your sus-picions?"

"In connection with that woman, I have no sus-picions."

"What then?"

"Convictions!" exclaimed the colonel.

"And you have good reasons for them?"

"The best in the world."

"Then, for Heaven's sake tell me and ease my heart. I am sure you will say nothing you do not know to be true."

"Nothing that I do not know to be true. Since you left Honolulu I have, with my own eyes, seen your precious friend, Captain Featherstone, kissing the wo-man who is making a fool of you."

"I can't believe it!"

"Then you mean to say I am willfully lying?" said the colonel, with a ring of anger in his voice.

"No, no, colonel, not that; only that you are deceiv-ing yourself," replied Kohala, in a voice trembling with excitement.

"Kohala, look at me and tell me how long you have known me."

Without looking, Kohala replied:

"As long as I can remember."

"Did you ever know me to tell a lie?"

"Never."

"Did you ever think my mind was not clear?"

"No."

"Do you think I can see you there by my side?"

"Surely."

"And you hear my voice?"

"I do."

"And I hear yours?"

"Yes."

"Well, just as clearly and distinctly I saw this man Featherstone kissing this adventuress, Mrs. Holmes, and I heard him telling her that as soon as his plans were perfected and you were declared king that they should leave Honolulu as man and wife."

"When was this?"

"The night before I left."

"And she seemed to consent?"

"Seemed to consent! When a woman offers no objection to such familiarity she consents," said the colonel, scornfully.

"Pardon me, my best of friends, if for the moment I should regard this as a horrible dream, said Kohala, with his hands pressed to his eyes as if to shut out the burning light. "It is all so unexpected that I cannot realize it. She told me that she loved me, and, loving her, I believed it. If, in truth, she has deceived me, then farewell to her and Hawaii."

"That is all nonsense, my son," said the colonel, with more kindness in his voice. "Every young man worth a snap has passed through the same experience. Some one has said, and I believe it, that the human heart is like a beef-steak—the more it is pounded the tenderer it gets. Of course, you feel mighty bad over this. I remember I did when, many years ago, I discovered that my best girl had betrayed me and run away with another man; but after a few weeks I got over it and was as good as new—better, indeed, for I had all the benefit of the experience."

"That may be," said Kohala, quietly, "but you are not a Hawaiian."

"Oh, nonsense! When it comes to love, human nature is the same all the world over."

The colonel threw away the stump of the cigar he had been smoking and fixed his eyes on the road in front, far down which he could see the white steeples shooting up through the palms that embowered Hilo. Kohala wanted to dwell on this subject, but as he could get no comfort from the man who had given him all this agony he lapsed into silence.

There was much that he had not told his friend, much that must yet come to his knowledge; yet he dared not speak, for he felt that if the truth were known the blow, which he did not fear so far as it threatened himself, would fall on the woman he loved.

He had all faith in Colonel Ellis, and believed him incapable of deceit or falsehood. He realized, further, that his guardian must have some ground for his charge; but if an angel had appeared and told him at that moment that Marguerite Holmes was false to him he would have treated the message with scorn and incredulity.

Curiously enough, while his love for the Englishwoman was strengthened rather than abated, and he still believed her entirely true and the colonel entirely mistaken, he suddenly conceived the most violent dislike for Captain Featherstone.

He could well see how Featherstone and every other man could fall in love with Marguerite; but, loverlike, it was entirely beyond his comprehension that she should love any man but himself.

At length the foaming horses were halted at the pier, where the colonel's steam-yacht was made fast.

Kohala's trunk was taken on board. Steam was up, and while a servant was walking the horses back to their stable the yacht was headed for the open sea.

As soon as the vessel was under way Kohala went to his stateroom and lay down. Some time afterward he was called to dinner, but he excused himself.

About ten o'clock that night a servant brought him in some tea and toast, but he could not eat it. Trouble is a great destroyer of appetite.

It was midnight before he dropped off to sleep. When he awoke the thumping of the engines had ceased, and, looking out through the port, he saw that the sun was well up and that the yacht was moored to her dock in the harbor of Honolulu.

CHAPTER XI.

PREPARING FOR THE STRUGGLE.

HONOLULU is never a bustling city, in the American sense. When the excitement caused by the Queen's purpose to force an unjust and illegal constitution on the people came to the knowledge of the citizens the city was in as great a state of uproar as Park Row, New York, on election night.

The natives, as if dreading an explosion, the reason for which but a few of them could understand, drew off by themselves and discussed the situation in whispers from the standpoint of their fears, for, though they would stand up for the Queen against the encroachments of the white men, yet they did not like her.

Bolder but equally cautious, the white population gathered in groups on the streets and discussed the revolution which all felt to be inevitable.

The office of the American Minister was crowded with merchants, his own countrymen, and many French and Germans, all pondering over what was best to be done to insure protection to life and property in the event of an outbreak.

By this time each side had decided on the course to be pursued, and as a result, Honolulu was in a state of calm that all saw was far more ominous than the first noisy and excited outbreak.

It was well known to the citizens, well known to the police, and, of course well known to the vigilant adherents of the Queen, who had now made the palace their headquarters, that bands of white men went nightly down the road to the race-track, where they threw out guards to prevent intrusion, and where it was believed Colonel Arthur Loring was drilling them, though as yet neither side had attempted to raid the arsenal, which it was well known both sides were watching.

But the present calm was ominous. It was such as comes upon the Hawaiian Mountains with the black clouds that tell of an impending storm.

The white, uniformed guard before the palace and the dusky policeman, pacing before the Parliament House across the way, seemed both absorbed in other matters than their immediate duties.

Since the inevitable split between herself and a majority of the foreign residents began the Queen had been seen but little on the streets, and then she was closely veiled and in a covered carriage.

During the day there were but few people seen entering or leaving the palace, but at night this seeming neglect was made up for.

It was well known that the police were devoted to Her Majesty, and so they were shunned by her opponents, all of whom were prepared to resist an illegal arrest.

But there were events of too much importance to the Queen to be kept from her knowledge till night.

Colonel Ellis's yacht, with Kohala on board, had scarcely been made fast to her dock when a young native, a clerk at the Government House, started for the palace.

The Queen was closeted with her minister, Mr. Eli Porter, when the clerk rapped at the door and was told to enter, for, though the sovereigns of Hawaii have tried to imitate the formality and exclusiveness of European rulers, they have never had the means to support such state, nor is it at all certain that their native adherents, who still retain much of the old clan spirit, would submit to it.

"Hello, Lan!" called out Porter, when the young man stood bowing and panting before Her Majesty, "what is up now?"

"Colonel Ellis has returned," said the messenger.

"Well," snapped the Queen, "there is nothing startling in that. As there was no good ground for hoping that Colonel Ellis might be drowned, we, of course, expected him back."

"But, Your Majesty," continued the messenger, "Kohala has come, too!"

"Kohala here?" exclaimed the Queen.

"Yes, Your Majesty."

"And he returned with Colonel Ellis?"

"He did, Your Majesty."

"Well, what do you think of it, Mr. Porter?" asked the Queen, as she turned and looked at her minister.

"I am not at all surprised," said Mr. Porter. "Indeed, I may say that I am glad." Then, to the messenger: "That will do, Lan; you can leave."

As soon as the young man had gone out the Queen said. rather petulantly:

"Why are you glad that the pretender is here, Mr. Porter?"

"Because here we can watch him, and hold him. Once under the control of Keona and his daughter, he would be out of our reach. Why, I think it shows bad generalship to fetch him here."

"They did not fetch him," said the Queen, with a grim laugh.

"Who brought him, think you?"

"Marguerite Holmes."

"I think Your Majesty is right."

"I know I am."

"Good; then if Marguerite Holmes can control him— and I think there is but little doubt of her power—we must see to it that the lady does not escape our influence," said Porter, and he rose and backed two steps from the Queen's presence, as if about to depart, when she gave her royal permission.

"Do you know, Mr. Porter, that I have recently changed my mind about this woman?" said the Queen, with the subdued tone of one about to communicate a secret.

Mr. Porter took a step nearer, and asked:

"In what way, Your Majesty?"

"I think she is weak and cunning."

"Does Your Majesty call that a discovery?" asked Mr. Porter.

"Not at all. But I have come to believe that she loves Kohala better than she loves any other being in the world, and that is a discovery."

"Her capacity for love, I imagine, is rather varied," said Mr. Porter, with a sneer. "But why should we care who or what she is, so long as she answers our purpose? On the whole, however, I should be glad to know that what you say is true, for in that event we can the better use her for our own ends. Now, with Your Majesty's consent, I shall withdraw, for it is possible that the dreaded raid on the armory may be made to-night, and I must be ready with our friends to see that the arms do not fall into the hands of the rebels."

"And you will avoid bloodshed?" she asked.

"If it can be avoided, Your Majesty."

And Mr. Porter left the palace and went over to the Government House, where he had an office, but where for some weeks there had been but little public business transacted.

He found a dozen men, nearly all "full-bloods" or half-breeds, awaiting him, and all looking as if they feared something serious might immediately happen if any of them spoke above a whisper.

Lan, the young man who had brought the news of Kohala's arrival to the palace, was present, and he had evidently reported the same thing, for they were discussing the matter and speculating as to what it portended.

Speaking in their native tongue—a language which

Porter understood quite as well as he did English—a tall, powerfully built Hawaiian, who was employed in the Queen's gardens and whose breath told that he had acquired at least one of the white man's most destructive vices, said:

"Why bother about this youth, Kohala? Why fear him when six inches of steel in his heart will put him out of the way forever?" and the man, as if to show that the blade and the arm to drive it were ready, drew from his belt a long two-edged dagger.

Porter took the weapon, tried the edges against the ball of his thumb, as some men try a razor before shaving, then said:

"Yes, with that, Hoi, a brave man could do the work; but if he was discovered, I wouldn't care to insure his life, so long as there are Americans in Honolulu."

"The man brave enough to do the deed will be too cunning to be detected; yet there will be a great risk, and it should be paid for. What say you to that, Eli Porter?"

"I say you are right. But put the weapon away. This is not the time or place to talk."

The man whom Porter called "Hoi" was sheathing the dagger when Captain Featherstone came in, looking very much excited.

"Mr. Porter," he began, "I must see you alone and at once!"

Mr. Porter led the captain into his private office, closed the door and asked:

"Well, captain, what is the new danger?"

"You know that this man whom they call 'Colonel' Loring, though of late he was known as 'captain,' is a trained soldier, a graduate of the great American military school at West Point?"

"I am aware of that," replied Porter, "but are you not also a trained soldier?"

"Yes; but my countrymen, the English, will not stand by me as the Americans do by Loring."

"The Americans are powerless, so long as they have no arms, and they cannot get arms while a hundred of the Queen's most stalwart adherents are secreted in the arsenal."

"Yet, Mr. Porter, they have arms!"

"You are sure?"

"I am certain."

"But, in the name of all that is reasonable, how could they get them in Honolulu without my knowledge? I have ordered all the stores that sell arms and ammunition to be closed."

"And they were closed, a fact that made it easier for the Americans to get all the pistols and ammunition they needed by the back doors. Then, men have been going on board the *Boston* in gangs of late, and it is believed they have brought away rifles under their long coats. Our Consul is certain that, at a signal to be given by the Americans on shore, the captain of the *Boston* will at once land his sailors and marines, seize the palace, supplant the Hawaiian flag with that of the States and depose Her Majesty by that act."

"And think you that the English captain and the English Consul will look idly on while that is being done?" asked Porter.

"They cannot help themselves. They dare not precipitate a war with the States."

"Then what would you advise?"

"That you precipitate the inevitable."

"In what way?"

"Show your hand and your force. There are five thousand men ready to oppose the Americans, and they will
do it if Kohala can be induced to lead them—"

"Which would mean that within twenty-four hours
Kohala would be proclaimed King of Hawaii."

"Better that than an American protectorate. You know
better than I can tell you that the days of the Queen, as
a ruler, are numbered. You and all her friends, even
Her Majesty, will reap the advantage of the course I
suggest," said Featherstone, with unusual energy of
manner.

"Which is to resign in favor of Kohala?"

"Exactly."

"And so ignore the Princess Kaiulani, whom she has
willed to be her successor?"

"As the will of the Queen is ignored by even her
friends it is better that she should make a virtue of
a necessity. The course I propose means success; any
other course is ruin."

"But could we get Kohala to agree to this?" asked
Porter, evidently impressed by the other's words and
manner.

"I can promise that."

"But why are you so sure?"

"I know Mrs. Holmes; she is my friend—"

"Every man's friend," sneered Porter.

"No, sir!" said Featherstone, hotly. "She is a lady,
and has no talent for deceit, any more than she has love
for the Americans. To keep Hawaii from their grasp
she is willing to use to the utmost the power she has
over Kohala. Whatever she advises he will do."

"The more fool Kohala. But I must have time to think over what you have said. I can do nothing without the concurrence of the Queen."

"But time is flying. There is not a minute to be lost. To-night, if ever, the blow for ascendency must be dealt!" said Featherstone, and he enforced his words with emphatic gestures.

"Good; then you bring me the assurance—and, mark you, there must be no doubt about it—that Kohala is ready to lead on our side if the Queen resigns in his favor, and then I will tell you our decision. At present we are beating the wind. Go to Mrs. Holmes at once and get her to secure Kohala's agreement in writing. That will settle matters," and Mr. Porter reopened the door leading into the general office.

Captain Featherstone replaced his hat and started out to where a closed carriage awaited him. He was evidently disappointed and angered at Porter's seeming indifference. He did not know that Porter clearly understood his purpose, and that he was quite as much opposed to the rule of the English as he was to that of the Americans.

"Where to, sir?" asked the driver.

"To Mrs. Holmes's," said Featherstone, as he sprang into the carriage and closed the door with an angry bang.

\

CHAPTER XII.

AN EXCITED MEETING.

It was the middle of the afternoon when Kohala and Colonel Ellis took dinner in the cabin. In his anxiety to see Marguerite Holmes he would have gone without his dinner; but he had sufficient self-control left, or, at least, so he imagined, to keep his feelings from his friend.

As if reading his thoughts, the colonel said, when they rose from the table:

"You must try to forget your own affairs for the present, and come with me to the Hawaiian Hotel. Our friends, many of whom have not met you, will be there, and let me say that your future success will depend on the impression you make, so try and banish this lady from your mind for the time being."

Kohala coughed and nodded to indicate that he fully understood what was expected of him and his own inability to realize it.

To "banish this lady from his mind for the time being!" Why, Colonel Ellis might as well have asked him to stop breathing for the time being, for the one would have been quite as possible as the other.

He had tried to banish her from his mind, but that very effort of will served but to make her the more fixed in all his thoughts.

His nature was romantic rather than heroic, intense rather than strong; yet its very weakness was due to the absorbing and engrossing fidelity with which he clung to the idol of his heart, believing that the woman whom he could so love must in every way be worthy of his adoration.

But he could not have felt this love and been incapable of jealousy. He was quite prepared to believe in the treachery of Captain Featherstone; but it would have been like a knife in the heart even to suspect Marguerite Holmes of treason.

Had he been a white man he would have doubted, or at least have investigated on less evidence; but in matters where the emotions were concerned he reasoned from his hopes, and all the innate impulses of his barbaric descent asserted themselves.

Without attracting attention he and Colonel Ellis were driven to the Hawaiian Hotel, on the broad veranda of which they found a number of United States naval officers, in white undress uniforms. These gentlemen bowed to the colonel, but did not try to stop him, though it was evident from the whispering that followed his disappearance with Kohala that they fully understood the purport of his coming.

Strolling about the ample, palm-shaded grounds there were a number of English naval officers in citizen's dress, smoking and chatting as if they had no other purpose in mind than to while away the hot hours of a tropic afternoon.

The officers on the veranda and those under the trees were most courteous to each other when they met, and when they stopped to chat they discussed everything but that which was uppermost in their minds.

The most optimistic could not hide from himself the fact that, within the week, the guns of their respective ships might be blazing into each other in the harbor of Honolulu.

The Council of Public Safety was in session in the upper room before referred to, and it was guarded by armed men within and without.

Although well known to these guards, the rules of the Council were so strict that the colonel could not be admitted till he had given the pass-word and countersign and vouched for the loyalty of his companion.

There were fully thirty earnest white men present, and, at sight of the colonel and Kohala, they rose to their feet and applauded, to show their respect and delight.

Kohala was personally introduced to all the men present whom he did not already know, and then he was given a seat beside the colonel, who took the presiding chair.

Mr. George King, who had been acting as president during the colonel's absence, saluted, and said:

"Colonel Loring was about to give us a report of the situation from the standpoint of a soldier; if our president offers no objections to this, it might be well for him to go on, for it is evident to all of us that the crisis for which we have been preparing for weeks has at length come."

"Colonel Loring's report will be in order," said the president, and he stilled the hum of voices by rapping with his gavel on the long table about which they were gathered.

Colonel Loring was in citizen's dress, but a uniform was not necessary to make him look what he was, every inch the soldier.

Rising, and occasionally refreshing his memory by reference to a note-book which he held open, Colonel Loring said:

"Mr. President, and gentlemen of the Council of Public Safety, it is hardly necessary for me to assure you that, since you placed me in command of the Provisional troops of Hawaii, I have done everything in my power to perfect the organization and to make it efficient."

He was interrupted here by applause, none the less hearty for its being suppressed.

"We have at present about five hundred men, fairly well armed and drilled, and twice that number who are ready to join us as soon as we need them. We need them now; but, without arms, they would be in the way and would only serve to add to our loss in the event of a conflict with the forces of the Queen."

"Where is the arsenal?" asked an impulsive Frenchman.

"Still in the hands of the authorities, or, I should say, it is in the keeping of the creatures of the Queen," replied Colonel Loring.

"Then why not take it into our keeping at once?"

This suggestion met with the same suppressed applause, and the men about the table nodded their approval.

"It is of that I would speak," said Colonel Loring.

"Go on! Go on!" came from all parts of the room.

"Our enemies are watching us—"

"We know it!"

"And if we do not seize the arsenal this very night and so precipitate the conflict, then the other party will do it, and they will be in a position to defy us."

"What force guards the arsenal?" asked Mr. King.

"It is supposed to be watched by some half-dozen soldiers; but, as a matter of fact, Minister Porter has been filling the place every night with a hundred or more men. A hundred such men, if properly approached, can offer no very serious resistance; but if five thousand men are gathered there it will be very different. I have learned the signal which the enemy propose to give when they wish to assemble their forces."

"What is it?" asked a dozen men.

"A beacon fire is to be lit at midnight on the crest of the Punch Bowl. For the past week but few of the Queen's adherents who are able to bear arms have gone to bed before morning," said Colonel Loring, referring for confirmation to his note-book.

" Why can we not have a force at the Punch Bowl to prevent the beacon?" asked the president.

"I have taken care of that," replied Colonel Loring, quietly. "Every night, under a cool, brave officer, a band of our best men have been concealed on the crest of the Punch Bowl. If the fire were started it would be at once extinguished, and rockets would announce to us that fact and the opening of the contest."

"In such an event," said the president, "what means have you taken, here in the city, to announce to our friends that the struggle has begun?"

"We have men stationed in all the belfries of the churches and on all the towers of the engine-houses. As soon as the rockets are seen the bells will announce the fact to our friends and they will assemble at places decided on, and under leaders who have my instructions as to what is to be done. I have taken every precaution, and I think you can trust me," said Colonel Loring, with the modest confidence that is ever the characteristic of innate military ability.

With the calmness but rapidity of action that distinguishes veterans under fire the Council hurried through a great deal of business, and at its conclusion every one present began to shout:

"Kohala! Kohala! Kohala!"

The young man had attended public meetings before, and so knew what was expected of him. In all that had been done and was being done by the men present he was in perfect sympathy; yet one may have a profound sympathy without being able, publicly, to give his reasons for the same.

Mastering his nervousness with an evident effort, Kohala rose to his feet, and, steadying himself by holding on to the chair on which he had been seated, he said, in the clear, melodious accents that were not his least charm:

"Gentlemen, I am a Hawaiian by birth and blood; but I trust that I am more than that, and that is, a man who is neither afraid nor ashamed to greet every other man, without regard to his race or nationality, as a brother."

A cheer, that could not be restrained and that must have been heard in all parts of the hotel, greeted this fine sentiment.

"I have neither the experience nor the wisdom to address men so much older than myself," he continued, "but I am not so dull as not to understand my country's present unhappy situation. Thanks to Colonel Ellis, I have been opposed to hereditary monarchs ever since I began to reason. This I say, though well aware that my own prominence in this movement is entirely due to the fact that, in line of descent, I am the rightful heir to the throne of Hawaii."

Again the applause broke out, and admiration glowed in the eyes of the men who heard the young orator. He went on:

"My rights to the throne I shall never press. I believe that all rulers should be elected, and Hawaii must
be no exception. To achieve this end, command my
fortune and my life; but, gentlemen, there is one thing
you must not insist on."

"What is that?" asked a member.

"That I shall help you to establish here a free republic, and that I shall inaugurate that republic by marrying
for reasons of State."

This produced some laughter and many questioning
looks.

"An alliance between myself and the daughter of the
chief of Hawaii might be good policy, as kings understand it. Mark you, the daughter of the chief is far
too good for me; but you should not insist on treating
me like the heir to a throne by selecting a wife for me,
when you tell me I am to be a free citizen in a free
land. My friends, that is all I have to say."

The applause broke out again when Kohala sat down,
and, while it was evident that a majority of those present indorsed his views, it was equally evident that all
were disappointed, for the allegiance of the chief Keona
who was not a republican, was essential to the success of
their plans.

Colonel Ellis admired the evidence of ability shown by
Kohala, though disappointed, and comforted himself
with the belief that the young man would change his
mind as to the daughter of the chief when he learned
for himself that the woman to whom he had given his
heart was entirely unworthy.

By the time the Council had ended its session night
had come to Honolulu.

Colonel Ellis told Kohala that they were both to remain at the Hawaiian Hotel, so as to be in a good position to receive reports and to direct affairs.

"I shall trust you to direct," said Kohala, with spirit; "that is the provence of mature men; but if there is to be action and danger I should blush for myself if I did not share it."

This was said in the presence of Colonel Loring, who, with Kohala and the colonel, was the only person present in the latter's room.

"Can you ride well?" asked Colonel Loring.

"I should; I began as a boy in the mountains of Hawaii, and I have never allowed my skill to lapse for want of use," replied Kohala.

"Then," said the colonel, "I shall feel glad and honored if you will serve on my staff to-night."

"But," joined in Colonel Ellis, "there may be danger."

"If there were no danger," said Kohala, proudly, "I should not care to serve."

"Spoken like a true soldier," said the gallant young leader of the Provisional army, as he shook Kohala's hand. "We can find plenty of men to sport uniforms and pose for the admiration of ladies when there is no danger; but the man who faces a danger for principle's sake—and the danger's sake—is a brother after my own heart."

"I shall not interfere with Kohala's purpose," said Colonel Ellis. "But you younger men must not forget that I, too, am a soldier, and so distinguish between duty and daring. The leader who unnecessarily exposes himself is not brave, but reckless. A general, unless the case be desperate and his example needed, should not lead a charge. The life of Kohala is of more importance to his country than that of a common soldier."

"Still the common soldier who risks his life for liberty is quite as noble a man as the general who commands him. For one night, at least, I shall be a common soldier, and subject to Colonel Loring's command," said Kohala, with an earnestness that had in it nothing of the braggart.

The three men had dinner together in Colonel Ellis's private sitting-room; but not one of them seemed to enjoy the meal, so absorbed were they in the events which the night was to bring forth.

Colonel Loring had a horse provided for Kohala, and he saw that there were pistols in the holsters and a good supply of cartridges in the young man's belt.

They bade good-by to Colonel Ellis, then rode down toward the race-track, picking up on the way other mounted men and many men on foot, all bound for the rendezvous where they had been assembling since the trouble began.

The stars were hidden by black clouds, as if the elements were in sympathy with the work to be done in Honolulu that night.

There were but few lights visible in private houses there were but few people on the streets, and a gloom that could be felt hung over "the Queen City of the Pacific."

CHAPTER XIII.

THE FIRST BLOW IS STRUCK.

THERE were guards all along the road to the race-track; but vigilant though these men were, they could not prevent the silent, swarming spies of the Queen from watching and reporting on their movements.

To-night there was less secrecy than heretofore. Both sides felt that the time for action had come, and that the next twenty-four hours would settle whether Hawaii was to be free or to remain under the arbitrary dominion of a monarch who, of her own volition, or through the ill-advised influence of some of her ministers, had chosen to ignore the rights of her foreign-born subjects and to trample under foot the accepted constitution of all her people.

To Kohala, who kept by Colonel Loring's side, it seemed as if the young leader had entirely changed his character since they rode into the darkness from the Hawaiian Hotel.

Ordinarily, Colonel Loring was the embodiment of courtesy; indeed, he was distinguished for his easy, graceful manners and the entire calm and self-posses-sion of his bearing; but while the latter had not left him, he was now quick and peremptory in his man-ner. His voice had in it a ring that insured obedience, and his every act told of a brain-directed energy that stirred his men and filled them with confidence, for soldiers, in or on the eve of action, ever admire a com-mander who can command.

Kohala expected that the colonel would form his men

into companies and march them directly down on the arsenal and storm it, if it were not at once surrendered; but in this he was disappointed.

Through a swarm of orderlies who stood ready to do his bidding the colonel assembled all his subordinate officers, and, as in the darkness he called each man by name, he gave him his special orders and saw before he retired that he understood them without fear of mistake.

As each subordinate was given instructions and told where he must assemble his men in the city, and what he was to do when the bells pealed forth their signal, he started off promptly to enforce the command.

In less than half an hour after their reaching the rendezvous, so perfect had been all the preliminaries, the organized troops, in small bodies and by different routes, were marching into the city.

"Now we are ready," said the colonel to Kohala, "let us ride back."

"But there are only a few men with us," said Kohala, as he looked about at the half-dozen silent, mounted men who remained behind.

"We have all we need now," said the colonel, calmly; "when we need more, depend on it they will be forthcoming."

They turned back to the city, the glow of whose lamps looked blood-red on the lowering clouds.

The other horsemen fell in behind, but not a word was spoken. The time for talk was past, and the hour for action had come.

The horsemen halted in a churchyard back of the palace and not a pistol-shot from the Hawaiian Hotel.

Here all dismounted, and they found men awaiting to hold their horses.

"Keep by my side, Kohala," said Colonel Loring, as a man came up with a dark-lantern and asked:

"Are you ready to go up, sir?"

"I am," said the colonel; "lead the way, Phipps."

The man with the lantern unlocked the church door, and, when the colonel, Kohala and the two men who were to act as a signal corps had entered, the door was closed again and the slide of the lantern thrown back, so as to show the winding stairs leading up to the steeple and belfry.

The steeple ended in a tower in which hung a bell, and as soon as the party reached the little platform at the end of the last stairs the light was hidden again.

Kohala looked over the rail, and the gas lamps and electric lights revealed the city at his feet. By the glare of the lamps before the Parliament House he could see the heroic gold and bronze statue of his famed ancestor, King Kamehameha, and his heart was stirred to emulation of that great chieftain's deeds.

The palace seemed to be wrapped in darkness; even the two lamps at the great entrance gate burned with a duller glow than usual.

The Hawaiian Hotel was, in contrast with its stygian surroundings, fairly ablaze with light, and Kohala could see the silhouettelike figures of men moving swiftly across the illuminated spaces.

Down by the piers and out in the harbor he saw the colored lights that marked the port and starboard sides of warships and merchant ships at anchor; and far out beyond all these he saw the phosphorescent glow of the breakers on the barrier reef and he heard the incessant and rhythmic booming that followed their recession and advance.

After this survey he faced to the north. In that direction lay the Punch Bowl, from which the expected signal was to come, and in which direction every face was turned.

But absorbing though the situation was, Kohala could not remain indifferent, even under such circumstances, to the one object that he could not banish from his mind. Soldiers on the battlefield, with the thunder of guns and the crimson carnage of death about them, have been carried in imagination back to the days of their boyhood, when they gathered wild flowers in the woods or followed the droning wild bee to her hive; but there was nothing so startlingly psychological in the thoughts of Kohala.

"If it were day," so he reasoned, "I could see the cottage where she lives." She was to him so bright, so self-luminous, that he felt pained to think that she must be in darkness, for he could not see the glimmer of a light in or about the place where she lived.

From his reverie—and in love reveries time flies fast and unnoticed—he was roused by the low hum of the voices about him, and he heard Colonel Loring saying to the man with the dark-lantern:

"Phipps, have you a watch?"

"Yes, sir," was the reply.

"Step down where the light cannot be seen and let me know what time it is."

Phipps descended the steps some distance, a flash of light came up and vanished, then he reappeared and said:

"It is just half-past eleven, sir."

"Another long half-hour to wait," said a man beside the colonel.

"Have patience," was the young soldier's laughing response. "You may have more to do than you can well attend to before the night is over."

"Ay, faith," said Phipps, who spoke with the accent of an Irishman, "and it may be that the man who'll live to see daylight may find himself dead."

Another man was about to speak, but checked himself, for suddenly a light flashed out from the dome of the palace and it lit up the standard of Hawaii.

This was unusual, for it had been the custom to lower the flag with the sunset gun, and Colonel Loring was more than ever confident that the Queen's adherents were on the alert, and that the hour for action had come.

Following the appearance of the flag above the palace a cheer, or, rather, a shrill yell, came up from the streets, and the pounding of galloping hoofs could be heard.

At this juncture a man, who had made his way up the dark stairs, found Colonel Loring and said:

"I am ordered to report, sir, that there is a great crowd of natives gathering about the palace."

"We must expect that. How about the arsenal?" asked the colonel.

"There is no change there, sir."

"Very well. Report to our friends to stand ready for the signal. They will hear it and see it within ten minutes."

The man crept down again, and the quick fall of his feet was still echoing in the steeple when an exclamation burst from the men whose faces had been peering northward for what seemed to them an interminable time.

"They've lit the beacon!" cried one.

From the head of the Punch Bowl a fountain of flame leaped into the sky, transforming the picturesque hill into a volcano, as it had been of old.

"Make ready the rockets, Phipps," said the colonel, his voice as calm as if there were no crisis at hand.

"All ready, sir," was the response.

Higher and higher rose the flames from the crest of the Punch Bowl, and again the shrill cheer came up from the direction of the palace.

"It's gone again!" cried a number of men, unable to suppress their excitement, for the fountain of flame died out as suddenly as it had appeared.

"Have the matches ready, Phipps."

"Ready they are, sir."

A few seconds of intense darkness over the Punch Bowl, then, like a pencil of light drawn swiftly against the black background of the night, a rocket rose up toward the lowering clouds, curved gracefully downward, then exploded, and was followed by a shower of globes, red, white and blue.

Two more rockets followed in quick succession. Then Phipps, under the colonel's orders, struck a match, and three rockets, with scarcely an interval of time between their appearance, shot up from the belfry and exploded directly over the palace.

"The bell, Phipps!"

The bell began to clang at once. A deep, hoarse cheer rang up from the streets. From tower and steeple other bells clanged out the alarm, and down by the shore there was seen a flash, followed by the ominous booming of a gun.

"Now for the arsenal! Keep close beside me, Kohala!" said the colonel, as, with lantern held high above his head, for there was no longer need for disguise, he led the way to the ground, while the bell kept up its clanging as if it had gone mad or was being rung by a madman.

"Keep the horses here; we shall not need them at present," said the colonel, to the men waiting below.

There was no excitement in his voice and no sign of nervousness in his manner, yet Kohala, who kept close to his side as he ran for the arsenal, could see by the light of the lamps past which they dashed that there was an awful, an unconquerable earnestness in the young soldier's face.

There was not a policeman to be seen. At the sight of the rockets from the steeple and the first clanging of the bells the bravest of them had vanished.

Bugle calls and hoarse commands down the side streets where the volunteers had been impatiently waiting, the quick tramp, as of trained soldiers, the galloping of orderlies and the frightened cries of women and children in the houses, told that the revolution, so long dreaded by the people of Honolulu, had come.

Colonel Loring took a position near the arsenal, but Kohala noticed that, since leaving the steeple, he had not issued an order, nor was there any occasion for his doing so. His orders were given in advance, and so perfect were all the details that his subordinates promptly marched their men to the places that had been assigned them, and there halted till they should hear the bugles sound for the assault on the arsenal.

Although the Queen's adherents had long been expecting this very thing it came upon them with all the force
of a surprise, for their work was checked in its very in-
ception by Colonel Loring's signal corps.

Had the beacon been permitted to burn on the hill for
twenty minutes, as its designers intended, the native
force and the foreigners who took the side of the Queen
would have rallied at the palace and marched at once
on the arsenal. But the extinguishing of the light and
the red glare of the rockets, with the answering rockets
from the steeple, and the clanging of the bells, with the
sudden movement of large bodies of armed men along
the streets, had a most demoralizing effect on the men
who, but one short hour before, were so confident of
success that they expected to see every objectionable
American on the warship *Boston* the following morning.

With his drawn sword grasped firmly in his right
hand Colonel Loring, now reasonably well assured that
he was master of the situation, advanced to the main
door of the arsenal and knocked for admission.

After waiting long enough for a response without receiving any, he rapped again, saying, at the same time:

"Open at once, or I shall break in the door."

"Who is there?" asked a man in the voice of a native.

"I!" was the response.

"Who are you?"

"Colonel Arthur Loring, of the Provisional Army."

"I know no such man nor no such army."

"Then you had better make our acquaintance. Come,
my man, I am in no mood for parleying."

"But I was placed here with my men to protect the
Queen's property," said the man.

"There is no longer a Queen in Honolulu," answered the colonel.

"Where is Her Majesty?"

"There is no such person as Her Majesty. Will you open?" and the colonel beat on the door with the hilt of his sword, while a dozen brawny men appeared with a beam which they proposed to use as a battering ram.

"Hold up! we surrender!" cried the man from within.

Following this, lights were seen inside the building, the massive door was opened and the native soldiers and a number of natives with a few white men, all armed, came out, one at a time, and by the light of the improvised torches of Loring's men they laid down their weapons and were placed under guard.

Again a bugle sounded, and the company that had been detailed to take charge of the arsenal after its surrender marched in while the others fell into line like veterans, and, with the colonel at their head, advanced quickly toward the palace, not many hundred yards away.

There was no longer a guard before the entrance. The lights were extinguished in the great hall, and a timid Chinese gardener met the colonel at the steps and said:

"The Queen, she not here."

"Where is she?" asked the colonel.

"She go way."

"Where to?"

"Me not know," whined the man.

"Go up," said the colonel, to one of his men, "and take down the flag of Hawaii."

CHAPTER XIV.

THE QUEEN STILL DEFIANT.

ONE thing that has favored the continuance of hereditary rulers is the fact that they have been credited with
qualities which they ought to have had, but which they
rarely, if ever, possessed.

Queen Liliuokalani might have urged her sex as a
reason to account for her want of physical courage
were it not that in times of great danger, and even in
the face of death, women who were not queens have
shown a nerve and undaunted front such as the bravest
man could scarcely hope to emulate.

The Queen of Hawaii committed the fatal blunder of
underestimating the force and resolution of her opponents, and of overestimating the strength and fidelity of
her adherents.

It has been said that any man will make a good soldier if well trained and properly led; but, with the
exception of the handful of palace guards, whose occu-
pation hitherto had been entirely ornamental, the
Queen's followers were untrained, and, still worse, she
had little politicians for leaders instead of resolute soldiers when the revolution came which she had herself
invoked.

It was the belief of Her Majesty and her friends that
there would be fighting at the arsenal and in and about
the palace; so, as a matter of prudence, she went in disguise to the house of a friend a short distance away, and
there confidently awaited the outcome of the struggle.

It had always been the custom, as with more powerful monarchs, to keep the royal standard floating over

the palace in the daytime when the Queen was present.
It was, no doubt, to create the impression of her presence after she had fled that some of her foolish friends
raised the flag at midnight and illuminated it with
lanterns for the delusion of the people—but it failed
of its purpose, if such was the intent.

From first to last it was never the purpose of the
Council of Public Safety to injure the person of the
Queen, nor, indeed, to shed a drop of blood unless its
army was assailed and forcedly resisted in the performance of duties demanded by the crisis.

In addition to the gallant Colonel Loring's personal
feelings in the matter the Council had commanded him
to protect, at every hazard, the person of the Queen; so
that she might have remained in the palace with perfect safety to herself and her household servants.

The Queen was anxiously awaiting the lighting of the
beacon fire on the Punch Bowl when Lan, the young
man who had brought her the news of Kohala's arrival
with Colonel Ellis, came into the darkened sitting-room
in the house to which she had fled and said:

"Your Majesty, it is as we have feared, Kohala is
with the insurgents to-night."

"How know you this?" she demanded, in an angry
voice.

"I saw him myself riding out with the man they call
Colonel Loring to the rendezvous at the race-track."

The Queen rose, and raising her arms tragically, she
cried out:

"Kohala is rushing to his own ruin fast enough; but
if I had true friends about me he would not be permitted to torment me in this way."

She waved her hand toward the door, and Lan vanished.

At the same time that she left the palace for this house the Queen sent for Marguerite Holmes, the messenger having orders to fetch the lady back with him.

Lan had just taken his departure when another tap was heard at the door, and Mrs. Holmes, very ashy and with a pained, anxious look in her eyes, yet entirely self-possessed in her manner, came in.

Hitherto the Queen had been effusive in her demonstrations on meeting the little Englishwoman; but now the savage, usually dormant in her passionate nature, asserted itself.

As if talking to a servant with whom she had good cause to be angered, the Queen said:

"I sent for you this afternoon; why did you not come to me?"

"I was absent at the time," said Mrs. Holmes, demurely.

"But you found my note awaiting you?"

The Queen plumped into the chair from which she had risen; but, although etiquette required that her visitor could not imitate the royal conduct without the royal command, Mrs. Holmes sat quietly down and said, with well-bred calmness:

"I was not at all well when I got home, and so I lay down."

"But you first read my note?" said the Queen, hotly.

"Your Majesty, I did not read your note."

"Pray why not?"

"Because it was not handed me till I got up."

"But you have a servant?"

"Yes, Your Majesty."

"And she knew the note was from me?"

"Only that it was from the palace."

"But that should mean me! You never had a friend at the palace but myself, and now you haven't one in it or out of it," said the Queen, hot with anger.

"I am sorry if I have angered Your Majesty," said Marguerite Holmes, rising with quiet dignity and adding: "You see I have obeyed your second request. Is it to pour your wrath upon me when others have excited it that you have sent for me?"

"No, it is not."

"May I ask the wishes of Your Majesty?" said the little woman, choking down a sob, "for I am still far from strong."

"Sit down!"

The Queen waved her hand to the chair from which Marguerite had risen. She sat down, interlocked her thin fingers, as was her habit when perplexed, and waited.

"Do you know," said the Queen, in a lower if not a milder tone, "that Kohala is now in Honolulu?"

"I learned it not an hour ago," replied Marguerite.

"From himself?"

"No, Your Majesty; from Captain Featherstone."

"Captain Featherstone?"

"Yes, Your Majesty."

"And you permit him to visit you still?"

"I cannot help it, Your Majesty."

"Why not?"

"Because he does not know my secret."

"Then he treats you as a lover?"

"As a friend."

"Friend!" sneered the Queen. "I am not a fool! I

have never liked your friend, for I know him to be what many people say you are."

"May I ask Your Majesty what that is?"

"An adventurer!" hissed the Queen.

Marguerite made an effort as if to rise. At the sound of the word "adventurer" she started like a spirited horse at the touch of the unaccustomed spur; but she restrained herself, though she could not trust herself to speak.

The Queen half closed her eyes, till they looked like two dark luminous slits, and the heavy lips were compressed, as if she were making an effort to control herself. At length she asked:

"Do you not think it strange that Kohala should come to Honolulu without at once calling on you?"

"In these troublesome times, Your Majesty, I do not know what to think," was the response, and Marguerite Holmes pressed her hands to her eyes and hastily withdrew them.

"Do you still believe he loves you?"

"I can see no reason for his changing," said Marguerite, the trembling hands again pressed to her eyes.

"Young men often have strange fancies, which they imagine to be love."

"So I have heard, Your Majesty."

"Mrs. Holmes?"

"Yes, Your Majesty."

"You must find Kohala at once and fetch him to me."

"But if I cannot do so?"

"Cannot! You must, or—"

The Queen hesitated, and the slits grew narrower and the compression of the lips gave her a fierce expression.

"Or what, Your Majesty?"

"Or I shall give your secret to the world. Now, find him and fetch him."

The Queen stood up, and Marguerite Holmes rose with an effort and tottered from the room.

As if her departure were the signal, rockets went whizzing into the air as soon as she had gained the street and all the church bells and fire bells began to clang.

Marguerite let fall her veil, while all about her she could hear the thunder of flying hoofs and the tramping of men. Shrill yells in the distance and hoarse cheers near by indicated to her the whereabouts of the rival factions.

Running rather than walking, and avoiding the illuminated places, Marguerite Holmes succeeded in reaching her cottage.

She found Clem awaiting her, and looking, as she always did, as stolid and sleepless as a sphynx.

"Get me a little wine, Clem!" gasped Marguerite, as she dropped into a chair and let her arms fall helplessly by her side.

Without any expression of sympathy in voice, face or manner Clem brought her mistress a glass of sherry, waited till she had sipped it down, then took the glass, and, turning it round between her thumb and finger, said, in her low, mechanical voice:

"He's been here to see you, mem."

"Whom do you mean, Clem?" and Marguerite looked up with more interest.

"The young, dark-complexioned prince."

"Kohala?"

"Yes, mem, and he was rare disappointed not to find you."

"Which way did he go?"

In her anxiety Marguerite rose to her feet and began putting on the gloves she had taken off.

"You told me not to say where you'd gone, mem, so, when he asked, I said I didn't know."

"What else did he say?"

"He asked if Captain Featherstone was in the habit of coming here very often."

"And what did you reply?"

"I said not too often to wear out his welcome, for he was a great friend and a countryman of yours."

"You should not have told him anything about it," said Marguerite, a faint flush coming to her cheeks.

"But it was the truth, and I could not help it. Oh, he's a rare fine gentleman, he is, even if his skin is dark, for he slipped a bit of American goold into my hand."

"And that was all he said?"

"Every word, mem."

"And he didn't say when he'd return?"

"No."

"Nor where he was to be found?"

"Not a word of anything like that, mem, I assure you," said Clem, as she backed to the door.

As Marguerite made no effort to detain her Clem kept up her backing till she had passed the door and closed it behind her.

She went to the little dining-room, but before setting down the glass in which she had brought the sherry, she helped herself to two glasses, draining each at a gulp, and muttering to herself as she did so: "Ah, me! this is a sad, sad, wicked world, and every one in it seems to be workin' for himself and not thinkin' of no' one else."

The person overhearing this might be led [to believe that Clem was herself a praiseworthy exception to the selfishness peculiar to all the rest of humanity; but, as will be shown, she was not beyond temptation, particularly when it came in the form of gold, for which she had the universal human fondness.

Waiting in the dark, for she had extinguished the light in her own room, till assured that her mistress was in bed, if not asleep, Clem crept softly out through the window that opened on the piazza, then, with a cloak about her gaunt form and a man's hat pulled down over her eyes so that her sex was disguised in the indistinct light, she made her way to the rear of the Hawaiian Hotel.

On nearing the place she slackened her pace and moved with more caution. At length a dark figure rose up before her, but, instead of being startled, she asked, without a tremor in the wooden voice:

"Is that you, Mr. Phipps?"

"Faith, me darlint," was the laughing response of the man who had guided Colonel Loring into the steeple, "it's mesel' and no one else. And it's tired enough I am waitin' here for you."

Phipps gave her his arm, led her into the hotel by the back way, and so conducted her to the chamber where the Council was in session.

CHAPTER XV.

WHERE IS KOHALA?

COLONEL ELLIS, with a half-dozen friends, was in the room in which the Council held its meetings, awaiting the outcome of the night's work, of which, judging by the confident expression on the faces of all the men present, no one seemed to entertain any doubt.

Every few minutes a messenger came in to report the progress of the men under Colonel Loring, and each of these confirmed the hope that the revolution would be as bloodless as it was wide-reaching in its effects.

Escorting Clem, Phipps, who had been elected a messenger of the Council, gave the pass-word at the guarded door, vouched for the fidelity of the strangely attired woman and entered.

As soon as the door was closed behind her Clem removed her hat from her stringy-looking head, threw her cloak over her arm, man-fashion, and bowed on rather stiff hinges to the gentleman at the head of the table.

The colonel had evidently met this strange woman before, for he nodded to her, just as if she were a man with whom he was forced to have unpleasant dealings, and, pointing to a chair at his left hand, said:

"Glad to see you are still alive, Mrs. Clem. Sit down, and tell me if this uproar has excited your nerves."

" I ain't got no narves," she said, grimly, whereat the men about the table laughed.

"That is the one thing"—the colonel was going to add, "and the only thing," but he did not—"that gives you an enviable pre-eminence over all your sex with whom

I have the honor to be acquainted. Nerve, Mrs. Clem, is an excellent thing in man or woman; but Heaven preserve me from people with nerves. Now, I suppose that little splinter of a woman, Mrs. Holmes, is just one bundle of parchment-covered nerves."

"It isn't that, sir; it's want of strength," said Clem. "But as to gettin' upset when there's trouble on I will say that she's just about as cool a hand as I ever met up with."

"Yes, Mrs. Clem, she is no doubt a very remarkable woman; but where is she now?" asked Colonel Ellis.

"At home and in bed, though I can't think she's so downright cool and calm as to sleep such a night as this," said Clem.

"And she called on the Queen to-night?"

"She did, sir."

"How did she seem when she came back?"

"She was right up and down rattled, and no mistake, sir."

"Did she have any callers during her absence?"

"Only one, sir."

"Who was he?"

"The handsome young dark gent."

"What! Kohala?"

"Yes, sir, that's his name, though I never can recall it when it's wanted."

"When was he there?" asked the colonel, his face growing very serious.

"Just 'bout half an hour after the bells began to ring."

"How long did he stay?"

"Only while I was tellin' him that Mrs. Holmes had gone out."

"Did you tell him where she had gone?"

"No, sir."

"But, of course, you knew?"

"I did, sir."

"And Mrs. Holmes seemed very much disappointed when she got back and learned that the young man had been there?"

"Yes, sir, she was that bad cut up that I had to fetch her some wine to keep her from swoonin' right off," said Clem.

Colonel Ellis stroked his forehead like a man much perplexed, then he called to Phipps:

"Find Colonel Loring at once, and ask him if he has seen Kohala within the last hour or if he knows where he is."

Phipps saluted and hurried out, and the colonel, after a further talk with Clem, gave her some money and dismissed her.

Within ten minutes Phipps, who had met Colonel Loring on his way to the hotel, returned with that gentleman.

"Why," said Colonel Loring, when he heard that Kohala had so recently called on Mrs. Holmes, "when we reached the palace I gave him a message for you. He must have passed Mrs. Holmes on the way thither and stopped in, for I recall that as I passed the cottage a short time before there were lights burning within."

"Well, he did not report to me," said the colonel, "and, knowing him as I do, I am sure that he would have done so if something serious had not befallen him."

"He was armed and knew how to care for himself," Colonel Loring ventured to say, though he clearly saw that this supposition did not eliminate the element of danger from the question.

"If a man were as strong as a giant and armed to the teeth," said Colonel Ellis, as if thinking aloud, "he might still be as a child before the dagger of an assassin."

"I think there is no need to be alarmed; still, if you say so, I shall have a search instituted at once," said Colonel Loring.

"I certainly do say so." Then, rising to his feet, Colonel Ellis added: "If any harm has befallen Kohala I shall demand an eye for an eye and a tooth for a tooth, if I have to shed royal blood in retaliation!"

Colonel Loring saluted, and went out, followed by Phipps.

The young soldier was not at all to blame for the absence of Kohála. It was to give him something to do as a member of his staff that he sent him with a message to the chief of the Council; and if Kohala stopped on the way, as he certainly seemed to have done, the act was in direct violation of his duty as a volunteer soldier, and such he certainly was for the time being.

As they hurried to the arsenal, about which most of the soldiers were now encamped, Phipps proved to be the most dismal kind of a Job's comforter.

"Do you know, colonel," he said, "what I've just been thinkin'?"

"What?" snapped the colonel, who was too busy with his own thoughts to care for those of any one else.

"That some of these Yalla Kanakas is mighty treacherous."

"So are some white men."

"Thrue for you, colonel; but most white min would give a fellow-mortal a chance to defend himsel'. Be-

gorra, I never did have no use for thim that has dark
skins."

As the colonel's only comment was a disapproving
grunt Phipps lapsed into silence.

The colonel found the men in camp about the armory
in high spirits. He had issued an order against drinking,
but the unexpected success of their venture had intoxi-
cated the men like wine, and so they laughed and
cheered and sang, and when the colonel came within
the light of the campfires they cheered him to the echo,
for, like a true soldier, he was very popular with his followers.

At sight of his face the uproar was stilled, for the
men were quick to see that something unusual had happened.

Calling the officers into the building and excluding
all others, the colonel told them that Kohala was missing and asked their advice in making a search.

One man said:

"Perhaps he has a sweetheart."

Another suggested:

"It may be that the young man got scared."

But the general opinion was that Kohala had either
been assassinated or captured and held for a reward.

"If it's for a reward," said one of the officers, "we
shall hear from his captors in the morning; but if he's
done for, why, it's my private opinion that we've seen
the last of him."

This view of the case, though warranted by the circumstances, was far from comforting to Colonel Loring.

"You, gentlemen," he said to the officers about him,
"have men in your commands who are entirely familiar
with every nook and corner of the city. Call these men

apart and tell them in secret what I want—that is, to find Kohala, dead or alive, and if dead, to secure those who were the cause. Mark you, there is not a moment to spare.''

The officers went out, and, within five minutes, returned to the building, each with from three to five men of his particular command.

Speaking in low, earnest tones, the colonel told the volunteers his reason for sending for them, and added:

"To the man who brings Kohala back, or reliable news of his whereabouts, I shall give from my own pocket a reward of one thousand dollars.''

Although this was not an overpowering inducement to any of them, all of whom were eager to assist their young commander, it can be said that the tendency of the reward was not to weaken their efforts or to dampen their ardor in the search. The men selected for this delicate undertaking were all Americans, and so accustomed to orderly methods of procedure.

One of their number, who at one time had been chief of police, and who was known as a detective of unusual shrewdness and one of the coolest and bravest men in the city, was elected to lead this extemporized organization for search.

This man's name was Blake, and he was slender and smooth-faced, slightly bald, and with a mouth that looked to be lipless.

Blake not only knew the city, but he knew all the shady characters in it. He had rare powers as a linguist, being able to understand the Hawaiians and to make himself understood in their tongue. He had the same facility with Portuguese, Chinese and Japanese, these nationalities being among those most prominently represented in the population of Honolulu.

In addition to these qualifications Blake was a man of energy, and he had a fine talent for organization.

He knew the worth of every man who had been detailed for the search, and knew just where to place him to the best advantage.

. Within a half-hour of Colonel Loring's return with Phipps to the arsenal Blake had mapped out his plans and dispatched the men to the different districts assigned them, telling them before they left to report to him from time to time at the Hawaiian Hotel.

"I thought," said Colonel Loring to Blake, when all the men had vanished, "that you would have gone out yourself."

"N—no," said Blake, shaking his head, "the time has not come for that yet, and I hope it may not come. I must get in the reports before I can act. It is as necessary to know what to avoid under these circumstances as it is to know what to look for. I shall sift all the reports, and if the young man is not found, then I shall put in my fine work. But let us get back to the hotel."

"You go to Colonel Ellis and tell him what I have done and what you are doing. I shall remain back till daylight, when I will detail guards to protect all the Government property in the city," said Colonel Loring.

Blake saluted, and hurried back, with Phipps, to the hotel.

The latter was stronger than ever of the opinion that Kohala had been done to death by "a knife in the hand of Yalla Kanaka."

Blake made no comment on this, but he had scarcely given his report to Colonel Ellis before an incident transpired that tended to give strength to the theory of Phipps.

The outer guard sent in word that a native, who was known to be in the employ of Colonel Ellis, wanted to see him.

"Admit him at once," said the colonel.

A young Hawaiian, dressed in a straw hat and the loose blouse and wide cotton trousers of a field-hand, came bashfully into the room, removed his hat and saluted his master.

"Well, Tom, what is it?" asked the colonel.

Speaking in fairly good English, Tom said:

"I heard, sir, that Kohala was missing.''

"Where did you hear it?"

"From two white men who passed me on the street not ten minutes ago, and who seemed to be sent out to search," said Tom.

"And you came to tell me this?"

"No, sir; to tell you what I know about Kohala."

"Go on! go on!" said the colonel, now sitting bolt upright and looking at the native as if trying to anticipate his story.

Looking into his straw hat, as if he saw there the source of his information and inspiration, Tom said:

"I know Hoi. Hoi is a Hawaiian and a bad, drunken man. It was this noon, and he was down by the water, sharpening his dagger, as if it was a razor. And I said: 'Hoi, why you do that?' and he say, 'to kill a man.'"

"Did he tell you whom he was going to kill?" asked the colonel.

"Oh, yes; for he think I am his great friend. He say: 'Tom, I get much money if to-night I kill a man. That man is young Kohala. Kohala, he troubles our Queen.'"

"And what did you do then?" asked the colonel.
"I do nothing; but I think Hoi, he's a great fool, and
he is drunk.   Then I think no more of what he say till I
listen and hear the two white men telling, that Kohala
he could not be found.   So, my master, I come to tell
you."

CHAPTER XVI.

MARGUERITE HOLMES LEARNS THE NEWS.

FOR its size, there is not in the world a more entirely
cosmopolitan city than Honolulu.

Here, the Chinese, Japanese and Portuguese outnum-
ber the natives and greatly exceed them in industry and
prosperity.   Here, also, are Africans and representatives
of all the islands of the Pacific, from New Zealand to
Formosa.   Every European nation is represented, and,
while in the main the whites are the best and the con-
trolling element, yet among that class is to be found the
most vicious and desperate criminals.

Although she had "left the palace" for what she
called "prudential reasons," the Queen, with more
spirit than wisdom, persisted in regarding herself as
the ruler of Hawaii; and she gave her orders, and persisted in giving them, till at length she realized that
they were not carried out, and then into her by no means
lucid mind the truth flashed that the Provisional Government, set up in defiance of her claims, was the sole authority to be obeyed in Honolulu.

The morning following the revolution the American
Minister, in order to secure protection to the property of

his own countrymen, called on Captain Wiltz, of the United States cruiser *Boston*, for assistance, and that gallant sailor responded by sending on shore a company of blue-jackets, armed with rifles, and under the command of prudent officers.

The sun was not an hour high before the flag of the Union was floating from the turret of the palace, for, by the act of the Minister, the Hawaiian Government was, for the time being, under the protection of the United States.

The Queen heard of this; indeed, she saw the flag as it went up, yet she comforted herself with the belief that the offense would not be permitted after her claims were made known to the American people.

"I shall again be recognized as the Queen of Hawaii." This is what she said to the many people who came to condole with her or to gratify their curiosity by seeing what a deposed Queen looked like.

Early the next morning she heard that a search was being made for Kohala, but she manifested no curiosity as to the reason of his absence, though it may be that she had this in mind when she dispatched a messenger for Mrs. Holmes.

Marguerite Holmes, though having much vital force and the resisting power that so often accompanies a high nervous organization, was far from being robust. Whatever extra effort she made was a draft on her resources, which, as is ever the case, had to be paid back to that inexorable banker, Nature, with compound interest.

It was near daylight when she dropped off into a troubled sleep, which might be described as unconsciousness rather than rest, for, as she rolled and tossed, she could still hear the whizzing of the rockets, the cheering of the troops and the still more alarming clanging of the bells.

When she woke it was near noon, and Clem was standing by the bedside with a cup of tea in her hand, the providing of which was the first service she rendered her mistress every morning.

Marguerite Holmes stroked her head and looked about her in that dazed, half-awake way of people who have not had enough nor the proper kind of sleep.

"What time is it, Clem?" she asked, when the fog had cleared from her still troubled brain.

"It'll be near noon, mem, I'm thinkin'," said Clem, "and I'd a-brought in the tea before, but I saw you were sleepin', and looked tired. I've got your bath ready, mem, and I'm shore you'll look as fresh as a pink after you're dressed."

This was a very long speech for Clem, who appeared to be in excellent spirits. Her mistress nodded, to indicate that her presence was not necessary, and then got up and made her toilet, taking little sips of tea in the pauses which her physical exhaustion made necessary.

Marguerite Holmes went through the motions of eating breakfast. Rather a lonely meal it was, but the woman, who was the soul of every gathering in which she found herself, led rather a solitary life, and loneliness is never so oppressive as at meal-times.

She had just finished, and her eyes began to grow a little brighter, when Clem, who had come in to take away the things, said:

"They had great carryin's on last night, mem."

"Was there bloodshed?" asked Marguerite, with a shudder.

"No, mem; that is, there was no right up-and-down

regular shootin' and stabbin', like I've heerd about in battles, where hundreds and thousands of men is killed; still they think there's been some one hurt."

"What do you mean?" and Mrs. Holmes pushed the ripples of bronze hair back from her broad, low forehead and looked more than ever like a girl in her teens.

"Of course, mem, you ain't heard that the Yankee sojers has took the town and put their flag up over the palace?" said Clem, purposely avoiding a direct answer, for she had something of the dramatic instinct in her mental make-up and wanted to work her information up to a fitting climax.

"I expected as much," said Marguerite, quietly. "But what about the bloodshed; who has been hurt?"

"They don't just know, mem, whether he has been hurt or not as yet, for they haven't been able to find him, with all their sarchin'."

"To find whom, Clem?" asked Marguerite, with increasing interest.

"The young gent."

"What young gent?" In her anxiety she fell into Clem's vernacular.

"The dark young prince—I can never recall his name —that is so fond of you, mem," and Clem smacked her thin lips as if the words had an unusually pleasant taste.

"Kohala!" exclaimed Marguerite, and the natural pallor gave place to an ashy hue, and the long-lashed gray eyes took on an expression of indescribable agony.

"Yes, mem, that's the one I mean."

"But what of him?" and Marguerite rose from her chair and looked into the stony eyes and stolid face of her attendant.

"The last thing that's been heard of him, mem, dead

or alive, was when he called on you last night and you
was out."

"Who told you this?"

"Oh, mem, detectives and others has been here, but I
told 'em you was sick. And they thought, fust off, that
you'd run away with him, till I let one man named
Blake look in the bedroom door and see for himself that
you was present and sleepin' like a little angel. But,
for all that, I'm shore there's detectives a-watchin' of
the house; but what they're doin of it for is more than
I can make out," and Clem actually smiled, something
that seemed to transform her into another but an equally
repulsive person.

Marguerite Holmes stood stroking her forehead like
one in a dream; all the light had gone out of her eyes
and her thin lips trembled and were bloodless.

Clem was beginning to feel alarmed at this awful silence, and was about to propose that she run across the
street and call in Dr. Wallace when the bell rang vio-
lently. She answered it, and came back to say:

"It's the same young man, mem, that's been here before from the Queen."

"Admit him," said Marguerite, hoarsely.

"Her Majesty desires me to say," said Lan, who, though
of graceful person, was anything but a courtier in his
manner, "that she'd like to see Mrs. Holmes just as
soon as she can come to her."

"Please say that I shall come at once," said Marguerite.

Lan vanished, and Mrs. Holmes went to her room and
put on the becoming little violet bonnet and a black lace
shawl—these things with no thought of effect, but because they were the first that came to hand.

"When will you be back, mem?" asked Clem, as her mistress stood at the door, in a weak, hesitating way.

"I do not know."

"But the captain, mem, he was here this mornin' and told me not to wake you, but I know he wants to see you very much. What'll I say to him, mem, if he calls, as he'll be most shore to do, for he seems to be very much troubled?"

"Say to him, also, that you do not know when I shall return."

"And must I say that you told me so?"

"You can, if you see fit."

"He may not like it, mem."

"Do as you are told, Clem; you are just a little bolder than I care to see you."

Into the sweet, troubled face there came for an instant a mingled expression of dignity and indignation that told more than volumes that the little woman had not forgotten in her anguish the lines that separated her from her servant.

Clem said: "Beg parding, mem," and stepped back, to choke her laughter with her apron when her mistress was gone.

Marguerite Holmes always wore a veil on the streets— one of those dark, spider-web things that neither conceals the face nor seriously interferes with the vision of the wearer.

Without seeming to do so, as soon as she entered the street from the garden surrounding the cottage she took a quick glance up and down. There were many men in sight, some of them detectives, no doubt, and she felt that they were watching her and discussing her; but she walked on seemingly indifferent to everything but her own torturing thoughts.

So far as it was known to her most intimate acquaintances in Honolulu there was nothing in this woman that indicated depth of feeling or seriousness of character. Indeed, if her best friend, Dr. Wallace, were questioned about it he would have been forced to confess, as a truthful man, that Mrs. Holmes gave those with whom she came in contact the impression of being light-hearted to the limit of frivolity, if not of flippancy; yet, with all this, there was a certain indescribable dignity about her in her lightest moods and most trivial times that indicated something better under the surface than appeared upon it.

Had Dr. Wallace seen her now, as she hurried toward the house where the dethroned Queen was stopping, he would hardly have recognized the pallid, drawn and pain-lined face for that of the smiling, sweet-voiced little woman who had thrown the net of her fascinations about him and about others, as more beautiful and more intellectual women could not have done.

Marguerite Holmes was more or less of a mystery to every one who knew her, but to not one of them was she so much of a mystery as she was to herself.

As drowning men are said, in the few seconds preceding unconsciousness, to see before their mental vision—like a landscape lit up by the lightning's flash on a starless, stormy night—the whole panorama of their lives, so she, as she hurried on, heart-tortured and seemingly with no destination in view, saw her own past, with its gloom and sunlight, its errors and its good alike, the results of unreasoning impulse.

Orphaned while yet a child; educated on the remnant

of a fortune left by a spendthrift father; married by stealth, and while yet a schoolgirl, to an Oxford student unable to pay his debts, much less able to support her, the sore trials of life came to her at a time when more fortunate girls retain still a fondness for their dolls.

All this she saw, as she had often seen it when she debated with herself the question of continuing the struggle. She saw her husband, whose education at the great English school had unfitted him for, rather than equipping him for, the battle of life, growing weaker and weaker through the excesses of his student life, which he had not the physique to stand nor the means to continue. After vainly trying to live as a coach for backward students, he was given a small annuity by a rich uncle and sent out to California to grow better, or to die; to the uncle, no doubt, the latter would have been preferred.

And so she saw herself a widow, with the small allowance continued. Her constitution, never strong, was shattered, and nothing was left but the indescribable charm that might have made her the ornament of a happy home and the wife of a worthy man.

All this Marguerite Holmes had kept to herself, for she had the secretiveness that is born of pride, and would have assumed an air of opulence amid penury and given the impression that she had been to a banquet when she was pinched with hunger.

Curiously enough this strange woman did not realize her one great weakness, and that was her desire to be admired, to make an impression on men, not so much for the sake of provoking love as to excite admiration, not so much to bring men under her influence as to feel that she need only be alone so long as she desired.

As a widow, she was enjoying the attentions which the insane folly of her early marriage had deprived her of as a girl.

She had never imagined what the love of a strong, ardent man could be till she met Kohala on the steamer that took her to Honolulu. His intellect and the grace and beauty of his person attracted her, for, though by no means well-educated herself, she had an intense admiration for men of culture and force; and in the contemplation of this 'superb young Hawaiian, with his manliness, his ardor and his frankness, she forgot all about the difference in race, as did all who came into contact with him.

Realizing her own dependence on the annuity that barely enabled her to live, and which would have been inadequate if she had not been so skillful with her needle as to obviate the necessity for a seamstress, it was prudent if not natural for her to treat the advances of Captain Featherstone with consideration, though, from first to last, she never regarded him with the feeling which she wanted to give to the man who took her first husband's place.

Kohala, from the beginning, she considered entirely out of her reach, and if she schemed to aid Featherstone it was with no intent to win at the expense of the young Hawaiian. All this ran through her mind, till she found herself rapping at the door of the house in which the Queen had found refuge.

───────

CHAPTER XVII.

CONTINUING THE SEARCH.

COLONEL ELLIS, in his anxiety for Kohala, forgot, for the time, the revolution which he and his associates had

set in motion, a revolution which was destined to make
an important, if not the most important, epoch in Hawaiian history

He had no sleep; but his was not an exceptional case,
for there were very few, but drunken men and children,
who went to bed in Honolulu that night.

Soon after daylight his daughter Alice, who, it will
be remembered, was betrothed to Colonel Loring, and
who acted as one of the Queen's maids of honor on the
occasion of the last ball given at the palace, came to see
him, with her mother.

Alice Ellis was an exceedingly pretty and attractive
girl, with the self-confidence and entire lack of self-
consciousness that are the distinguishing traits in the
character of the typical American girl. Ever since her
earliest childhood Alice had known Kohala. He had
been her playmate, and, with a childlike indifference to
race, she grew to regard him as a brother then, and the
years had strengthened rather than weakened this delightful sisterly affection.

Anxiety for the safety of her father and her lover, of
which Colonel Loring, with great thoughtfulness, kept
her apprised from time to time, kept her and her mother
awake all night; for, though by no means timid women,
they could not remain indifferent to the danger when the
coolest and wisest men in the city feared that their purpose could hardly be achieved without bloodshed.

The delight of Alice Ellis and her mother at hearing of
the great success of the revolution was quickly changed
to pale-faced grief when the colonel explained his own
haggard looks by telling them of the inexplicable absence of Kohala.

Mrs, Ellis was "certáin that that designing woman,"

meaning Mrs. Holmes, "was at the bottom of it." But
her husband, who had been of the same opinion, told
her that Mrs. Holmes, evidently a sick woman, was at
that very moment asleep, or at least in bed, in her own
room, and that her cottage was being watched by the detectives.

Alice Ellis was nothing if not just. She had had her
own doubts as to Mrs. Holmes, but she was too noble-
minded to breathe these doubts to another, and too generous to restrain an innate impulse to defend those who
aped the evil-minded by baseless denunciation.

"I have not seen a great deal of Mrs. Holmes," she
said, "but what I have seen I have liked. Poor little
thing! she may possibly be what we very good and
proper people call imprudent, but she is all alone, with
a thousand to criticise and slander and not one, that I
know of, to whisper to her a friendly word of caution.
I have noticed, and it has pained me to see it, that women who pose as models of all the proprieties watch
the little widow, not that they may discover what is
good in her, but that they may find something to distort
into a scandal."

"I am glad she has one champion in Honolulu," said
the colonel, not at all displeased at the position his
daughter had taken.

"I quite agree with Alice," said Mrs. Ellis, who, at
heart, was one of the best of women; "but she must
confess that Mrs. Holmes has been, to put it mildly,
most imprudent in her flirtations with poor Kohala,
who, in matters of the heart is as innocent as a child."

"My precious dearest!" said Alice, and she threw her
right arm about her mother's neck and kissed her, "in
matters of the heart, as you call love, we need no long

experience. Isn't Cupid pictured as a blind boy? He
would be a disgusting little cad if he went about with
his eyes open and wearing a dress suit. But pray, if
Mrs. Holmes loves Kohala and Kohala loves her—as
he certainly does—I can't for the life of me see what
moral code either or both of them is violating in that.
Love is natural, and must be expressed. As to this
baby-betrothing of Leila and Kohala, it is something
peculiar to Congo savages and European princes, and I
am astonished that my good, kind, noble, darlingest
papa should lend himself to the perpetuation of such a
disagreeable Kanaka custom. I wonder how he would
like it if some one had come along about the time he
was geting up courage to propose to you, mamma, and
told him that he mustn't do anything so wicked, for he
was betrothed to another girl while he was yet in short
skirts?"

"But Leila loves him," broke in Mrs. Ellis.

"Well, that shows more taste than spirit in Leila.
Why—and I say this knowing that she is a fine girl of
whom I am very fond—ever since Kohala has come back
she has figuratively and literally thrown herself at his
head. That's enough to frighten off any man, and much
more one who is inclined to lean the other way. She
should have concealed her love till she was sure of him—"

"As you did with Arthur Loring?" said the colonel.

"Exactly: that is an excellent illustration. Why, I
kept that man on thorns for three months, and all the
time I loved him quite as warmly and sincerely as Leila
of Hawaii can ever love Kohala. If this is to be a free
country let people marry for love and not for reasons
of State, say I."

"And so say we all of us," said Colonel Loring, who

had come into the room unnoticed while Alice was giving such free and eloquent expression to her views on
matrimony.

Colonel Loring, in response to a torrent of inquiries,
said that he had learned nothing more about Kohala.
Blake was now out, and the town was being thoroughly
searched, and all the roads leading from it were guarded.

He advised Colonel Ellis to go home to breakfast with
his wife and daughter, saying that he would remain
back at headquarters to attend to anything that might
turn up.

This suggestion was acted upon at once, and, weary
in body and tortured in mind, Colonel Loring threw himself on a sofa. Though his reason told him he was in
no way to blame, he still felt, as Kohala had been in his
charge, that he was responsible for his safety.

"I think, colonel, that if you could manage to swallow
a glass of good whisky that it'd aize yer mind and give
you an appetite for the breakfast," said Phipps, the glit-
ter in his eyes and a certain hesitancy in his speech telling that he had himself been testing the merits of his
own prescription that morning.

"No, Phipps, I want no whisky to provoke my appetite, nor do you, either. And, let me say, my good fellow, that the first man I find under the influence of liquor
in my command I'll make an example of."

"And, sure, it's dead right ye'll be, colonel. I am an
owld sojer mesel', and jooty's jooty, and I'd be for
hangin' the man that got drunk in the face of the inimy;
but in a time of pace, such as the prisint seems to be,
it's a intirely different thing." And Phipps saluted
in good military fashion and went down to order the
colonel's breakfast.

Colonel Loring had just about concluded the morning meal when Blake, looking as fresh as if he had not been up and at work all night, came in.

"Well, Blake, what news?" asked the colonel.

"We've found Hoi," replied Blake.

"For Heaven's sake, Blake, go right on and tell me all about it. I am too nervous to ask questions," and the colonel handed Blake a cigar, lit one himself, and again stretched out, full-length, on the sofa.

"I know Hoi," said Blake, as he bit off the end of his cigar and struck a match. "He's a lazy, drunken loafer, without the courage of a mouse or the conscience of a hog. We found him drunk down in the Chinese Quarter, as I expected, and he had his famous dagger still in his belt. It is as bright as it was the day he bought it. Of course, he might have done work with it and cleaned it after; but I am sure he wasn't sober enough last night to do that, or anything else."

"What did you do with the fellow?"

"Sent him to the lockup to get sober, which won't be till this afternoon, and then I'll frighten him out of the little wits he has left; but, as I said before, I am sure he's not in this job," said Blake, and he struck another match and pulled till the cigar was smoking to his satisfaction; then he changed his position and his manner, and asked:

"Colonel, what do you know about the man who calls himself 'Captain Featherstone, late of the English Army'?"

"Only that he became acquainted with Kohala in Europe some time ago, and since then, it seems, he has stuck as close to him as if he were his shadow."

"Was he in Kohala's employ, think you?"

"No, Blake, I am very sure he was not. I think, however, from the fact that he hangs round the English Consulate a great deal, that it is possible he is in some way in the employ of that Government."

"Yes, I have thought as much myself," said Blake.

"But why do you ask about Featherstone—surely you do not associate him in your mind with the abduction of Kohala, if, indeed, he has been abducted?" and the colonel sat up and flipped the ashes from his cigar.

"Colonel Loring," said Blake, speaking very slowly and with his face turned to the ceiling, the better to blow out smoke-rings, "I don't know much about diplomacy, I'll confess; but, like all men, I have my own opinions, even about things that are a bit hazy in my mind. But you are a graduate of West Point and know everything—"

"You are far off there, Blake; but go on," said the colonel.

"Now, don't you think if the English Government had the slightest ghost of an excuse for seizing on to these here islands that they'd do it at once and take the consequences?"

"Yes, Blake, that has been England's habit, and as a consequence she has gathered to herself more real estate than is profitable or that she can well take care of," said the colonel.

"Yes; but she ain't got anything finer than these islands, for God's sun in the twenty-four hours don't shine on a fairer or a richer land than this, except it might be on the green hills way down in the heart of Kentucky, where, to my mind, the Garden of Eden was originally built, or if it wasn't, it must have been an oversight. Now, if England wanted to get these islands in what

might look like a fair deal how do you think she'd go
to work about it?"

"Upon my word, Blake, I can't imagine, unless she
seized them by force, and that would mean a row with
Uncle Sam."

"No, she doesn't want a row; but how would this
work: Kohala, he's the rightful heir to the throne—
that we all know—but he doesn't want it; if he did,
nine-tenths of the natives would side with him. But
suppose he was made a prisoner like, and he was told:
'You must declare yourself King of Hawaii at once, or
die,' the chances are he'd proclaim himself—I know I
would. Well, the natives stand by him and England
shouting 'Fair play, and give the boy a chance!' comes
to his help. Why, then the game would be in England's
hands, and the King would soon find himself a puppet."

"That's a bold theory, Blake, and it shows you are
more of a diplomat than I am," said the colonel.

"There may be nothing in all this, mark you; but I've
made up my mind to watch Featherstone. He's playing
for big stakes, but I am satisfied that he has a job contract and is not regularly employed by the English Government. They couldn't afford to do that, but there is
nothing to prevent their handsomely rewarding the man
who turns over to them the King and Kingdom of Hawaii. That's what I've been ciphering out. That's why
I think Featherstone has been sticking to Kohala closer
than a brother. And that's why I'm willing to bet, even,
that when we come to make the last analysis of the situation—as the assayers have it—we'll find that this Featherstone is responsible for the absence of our friend," and
Blake lit his cigar again, while the colonel surveyed him
with undisguised admiration.

CHAPTER XVIII.

A STORMY SCENE.

CAPTAIN FEATHERSTONE was quite as · unpopular among the men of Honolulu as Marguerite Holmes was with the women. To be sure, he had been invited to dinner on board one of the English ships, and he had his mail addressed to the care of the English Consul, things that gave him a shadowy social standing, as did the fact that he and Kohala were, seemingly, intimate friends. Yet there was a something about Featherstone that provoked dislike and distrust, though his bitterest hater, if called on for a reason for his dislike, could have been forced to confess that he had no tangible reason, and he might quote the old rhyme:

" I do not like you, Doctor Fell,
But why it is I cannot tell;
Yet there is this I know full well—
I do not like you, Doctor Fell."

Captain Featherstone's attentions to the little widow did not escape the alert vigilance of the gossips of Honolulu—gossips who are the curse of every isolated community between the Poles and the Equator. Some actually believed that the two were actually married, and that the fact was kept from the public the better to enable them to carry out their schemes for despoiling it.

Featherstone, while defying the purpose of the Americans to force the Queen from the throne, was far too shrewd to openly take sides with Her Majesty or personally to oppose the forces organized by Colonel Loring.

Marguerite Holmes was not a strong woman nor even a self-reliant one; had she been either, she would never have permited herself to be brought so entirely under the influence of a man whom, at heart, she thoroughly disliked, and, as a consequence, dreaded.

The fact that she was a stranger in a strange land and that Featherstone was her countryman—and in a strange land a countryman seems like a kinsman—might be urged as an excuse for her treatment of this man. She was far too intelligent not to see through his purpose, and far too cunning to lend herself entirely to his schemes, though she had the tact to keep these thoughts to herself.

Marguerite Holmes did not know anything about the fate of Kohala, and this added to her torture; but from the instant of the first information she had, without Blake's shrewd method of reasoning, reached exactly the same conclusion.

She called upon the Queen, and found Her Deposed Majesty even more defiant and arbitrary than had been her habit.

Without any salutation, and scarcely deigning to look at her little visitor, the Queen ordered the others present to leave the room, and the door had hardly closed behind them when she asked, with maddening rudeness:

"Woman! what have you done with this man?"

"Pardon me, but I fail to understand Your Majesty," said Marguerite, and she looked down on the Queen, who remained seated, with a look of undisguised contempt in the long-lashed eyes.

"Where is Kohala?" demanded the Queen.

"I do not know," said Marguerite, with forced calmness.

"You don't?"

"I do not."

"And you wish me to believe that?"

"I wish Your Majesty to believe nothing You have seen fit to speak to me in an insulting way and I choose to answer as becomes a lady."

"You grow defiant because you think I am no longer the Queen of Hawaii: is that it?"

"That is not it. Your being a Queen did not elevate your character, nor can the loss of your throne degrade it. I speak to you now as woman to woman, and I repeat that I do not know what has become of this man."

"And yet the last time he was seen was when he called at your cottage."

"So I have been told."

"And you did not see him?"

"I did not."

"May I ask why?"

"Because at the very time he called I, though it was not an hour for an unprotected woman to be on the streets, yielding to the urgent summons of Your Majesty, came here," said Marguerite, with a dignity that was in striking contrast with the Queen's bruskness.

"I suppose I must believe you," snapped the Queen.

"Your belief in this and in all other matters is one of the prerogatives of which the revolution has not deprived Your Majesty. I should prefer that you believed the truth, for your own sake, rather than the error for my own."

"Mrs. Holmes," said the Queen, with a calmer manner. that rather intensified the tigerish gleam in her half-closed eyes, "you no doubt imagine that the ceremony performed at the palace on the eve of Kohala's departure for Hawaii was a sham?"

"Your Majesty led me to infer that it was a sham, and

that my concurrence was necessary as a matter of diplomacy; but I do not think I was deceived, and, let me add, I am responsible for my own part in that transaction and am quite ready to face the consequences. And now, if Your Majesty has no further degradation to offer me, I shall ask permission to retire," and, before the Queen, who was choking with anger, could make a reply, Marguerite Holmes was at the other side of the door and out of the house.

The little woman withdrew from this strange interview feeling that she had not had the worst of it; and, although she had been inclined to side with the Queen's party, her heart now throbbed with genuine satisfaction as, on the way back, she saw the United States flag floating from the roof of the palace.

On reaching home she went at once to her own room, and was in the act of exchanging her street dress for the warm-colored wrapper that so well became her slender figure when Clem rapped at the door, and, with a forced little cough, such as she always prefaced an announcement with, she said:

"Please, mem, the captain is here."

"Captain Featherstone?" Marguerite mentioned the name, although there was no other captain among her acquaintances in Honolulu. "Show him into the sitting-room, Clem, and say that I shall join him presently."

"The sitting-room, mem?" said Clem, in surprise, for heretofore the captain had been received in the little gem of a boudoir, which Marguerite had daintily decorated with her own hands, and where she sewed and entertained her few lady callers.

"I said the sitting-room," repeated Marguerite, with

an emphasis that surprised Clem, who had come to believe that her mistress was as wanting in force as a
child, and for which reason she held her in contempt,
for the woman was of that servile class that impose on
weakness and cringe before strength.

Captain Featherstone had been up all night, and he
looked as if he had not been in bed for a week.

He was pacing the floor and stroking his mustache in
a nervous way when Marguerite entered. His back was
toward her when he heard her light steps, and, turning
with extended arms, as if he were going to kiss her, he
said:

"Flossy, I am glad to have found you in at last."

She drew back from his advance, motioned him to a
chair, and, taking one herself, said:

"I have been here continuously, except when obeying
the commands of Her Majesty to call on her, which I
have done for the last time."

Featherstone, with an expression half angry and the
other half perplexed, eyed the little woman over, and
then asked:

"What is up with you?"

"Everything," she replied.

"What do you mean, Flossy? Surely you are not provoked at me?" he said, with forced calmness and something of the old gallantry in his voice and expression.

"No," she replied, "I am provoked at myself."

"But what for?"

"For being a fool and a tool, when all my instincts
plead that I should do right and be true to myself. But
the mischief is done; the milk is spilled, and crying will
not restore it."

"Oh. come, come, you are nervous, and no wonder

after the excitement of last night. The Yankees have started a blaze that won't go down if they want it to. They imagine that they have everything their own way, but they will see they are counting without their host."

Featherstone waited, and Marguerite, seeing that some comment was expected, said:

"I do not understand it; I might if I were a man."

"But you fully understood the plans, as I laid them down to you from time to time. I am quite sure of that, and let me say my plans have not changed," said Featherstone, confidently.

"Not changed!" she echoed.

"Not in the slightest."

"Then the revolution, as they call it, has not effected them?"

"On the contrary, it has helped me."

"You surprise me."

"Yet it is true; and now all I want is that you shall give me your influence for a few days and we shall have everything just as we want it."

"I may be stupid, but I must confess I do not understand."

"Then I shall make myself clearer."

"If you can."

"You remember our plan—"

"Your plan, captain," she interrupted.

"Well, my plan, if you will have it so, to get Kohala to have himself proclaimed king, which he can be made to do only through the unbounded influence you have over him. The time for this has come, and nine-tenths of the natives and a majority of the whites are ready to sustain him, if he says the word. And now—"

"And now," interrupted Marguerite again, grief and

indignation mingling and glowing in her eyes, "there
is one thing—and that the most essential—wanting to
perfect your plans."

"What is that?" he coughed.

"Kohala!"

"Kohala?"

"Yes."

"I will not pretend to say that I do not know the
young man is missing; but if I wanted to find him—
and I shall want to find him if you are still ready to
co-operate with me—I do not think there will be much
trouble in doing so."

"Then Kohala is living!" she cried, and she clasped
her hands and half raised them, as in the act of prayer.

"I feel very certain that he is; sure of it, indeed."

"And he is remaining away of his own volition?"

"Well, hardly that. His friends—and, mark you, I
am telling you this in the strictest confidence—are keeping him away from the Americans, and will continue to
keep him till he is ready to act; and he will be ready
to act as soon as you tell him what to do."

Marguerite Holmes interlocked her fingers while
Featherstone was speaking, and the little mouth worked
as if in effort to keep back the words that demanded ut-
terance. At length, unable longer to control herself, she
sprang to her feet and cried out:

"Take me—take me to Kohala at once!"

"Why, you are surprisingly eager," said Featherstone,
and the veins along his thick neck began to swell. "What
is the reason for this unusual interest in the young man?"

"It is the best reason for interest that any woman can
have," she said, and, with a glow of pride on her face,
she looked straight into his blood-shot eyes.

"May I ask what that reason is?"

"You may."

"Then I do ask it."

"The reason is that I love him as I never loved man before! Love him as a woman should love the man to whom she is lawfully wed!"

CHAPTER XIX.

A VERY IMPORTANT QUESTION.

THE simile, "like lightning out of a cloudless sky," is trite but very effective, considering its basis in fact; but that and all other stock illustrations intended to picture intense surprise and indignant amazement would be entirely ineffectual to give an idea of Featherstone's astonishment when Marguerite Holmes, looking straight into his eyes, told him that she loved Kohala, and that she was his wife.

Captain Featherstone was the embodiment of selfishness. It is doubtful if he ever performed a generous act from a noble motive. He would have been as ready, for a price, to sell his country as he was to aid her; and he would have promised marriage to the most wrinkled and toothless hag in Hawaii if, by so doing, he could further his own debased ends.

For two years he had been a follower, a hanger-on of Kohala, his purpose being to see him crowned King of Hawaii, while he himself—by what means we cannot pretend to say or by reason of what understanding— would secure a rich reward if he secured an English protectorate of the islands.

As far as he was capable of loving any one Captain

Featherstone loved Marguerite Holmes, and, as his wife, he may have been willing to share, in part, with her the money he expected to get; yet, like the mercenary and unprincipled wretch that he was, he brought Kohala under the fascinating spell of the woman he imagined he loved himself, till the entanglement became inextricable.

That Marguerite Holmes encouraged him in the belief that his attentions were agreeable and that she led him to believe that she would help him to carry out his designs, and on their completion become his wife, cannot, perhaps, be truthfully denied.

But in extenuation of this it should not be forgotten that the little woman was alone in the world, her sole dependence a petty annuity, the continuance of which rested with an eccentric man, whom she hardly knew and to whom she was allied by no ties of consanguinity.

While her conduct cannot be defended from a high ethical standpoint, before we condemn we should recall that she was like the proverbial drowning man, who, in his desperate struggle for self-preservation, forgets the rights of others in his fear of death. From the imposition of pretended love, which Featherstone implored her to practice on Kohala, she stood exonerated by her conduct.

Before Kohala went to Hawaii to visit the chief Keona, unknown to Featherstone a marriage with Marguerite Holmes was performed at the palace. The Queen's party, who brought this about, kept the matter secret, intending to spring it on the people if an attempt were made to place Kohala on the throne.

The Queen's friends knew that the knowledge of such a marriage would alienate the natives and provoke the relentless opposition of Keona, who, as has been seen, regarded Kohala as the betrothed of his daughter Leila, and with the chief's opposition the young man's chances as a ruler were a thousand times less than those of the deposed Queen.

Featherstone's purpose was to get Kohala to assert his rights to the throne, for which he did not care and which he would not have, unless it were to please the woman for whose gratification he was willing to sacrifice even life itself.

But when the captain saw all his airy castles dissolving before his gaze, and all his dreams of wealth dissipated by the very person on whose co-operation and fidelity to himself so much — everything, indeed — depended, he could not, for the time being, credit the evidence of his senses.

Forgetting the forced gallantry that had hitherto distinguished his intercourse with Marguerite Holmes, he shot out a fierce oath, and leaping to his feet, with arm raised as if he were going to strike her, he shouted out:

"Love! Lawfully wed! Woman, what do you mean?"

She looked so pale and delicate and slender as she stood there before him that Clem—who was screwing her eye to the keyhole outside—expected to see her mistress fall down in a faint, or, at least, to hear her scream; but instead, she never moved, never dropped her gaze from his red and brutally enraged face.

In a voice whose low, well-bred tones were in striking contrast with the fierce bellowing of the man, Marguerite said: "I mean what I have said."

"That you love Kohala?"

"Ay, every hair in his head and every curve of his face."

"And you are married to him?"

"I am."

"When did this happen?"

"Go ask Kohala. He does not lie, nor offer an insult to women who lack the brute strength of the bully. He will tell the truth, as becomes a man who is a prince and a prince who is a man."

Again Featherstone began pacing the room and pulling at his red mustache, while he shot glances at once questioning and malignant at the little woman. After a few minutes he came to a sudden halt before her and burst out:

"Merciful powers! you cannot mean this. You planned this fiction to tease me, to try me, to test me! Tell me that you did not mean it. Do that or lay me dead at your feet, for you might as well kill me in one way as in another!"

"Take me to Kohala at once, and in my presence let him speak for himself. If he says I have not told the truth I will confess that I have lied. If he says he wants to be King of Hawaii I will sustain him. If he says that henceforth he must live impoverished and in exile I will share his lot, and deem a cabin and privation heaven so that he be there."

Once more Featherstone resumed his pacing and his pulling and biting at the red mustache. Gradually the terrible truth found a resting-place in his fevered brain and forced upon him a realization of his own helpless and dangerous situation, now that the ally on whom he had counted for so much had deserted him.

Fears for his personal safety banished from his mind the fortune which he had imagined within his reach and the wife and houses that he was to count among his personal assets when he returned to England.

But he was quick to see that the woman who had blasted all his schemes had it in her power to have him arrested by the Provisional Army and subjected to the sanguinary rage of men, many of whom, in the gold hills beyond the sea, had given work to a coroner's jury for offenses mild compared with that of which he knew himself to be guilty.

Had he obeyed the impulses of his own cowardly and intensely animal nature he would have sought to coerce Marguerite Holmes into silence by intimidation and playing on her fears; but the unexpected rôle in which he now saw himself, and which was not the least element in his surprise, convinced him that it would be good policy to win her to his present purpose by means similar to those employed when he flattered himself that he was gaining her love.

With a sigh, which there was no need to affect, Captain Featherstone seemed to shrink into himself, for his head was bowed and his arms hung heavily by his side as he again halted before her and said:

"You have ruined all my prospects, and now, if you so desire—and I shall not ask you not to do so—it is in your power to hand me over to the lawless mob which is at present in possession of this unfortunate city, and let them tear me to pieces."

"I have no desire to do you an injury," she said, and her sensitive sympathies—her weakest characteristic—brought tears to the long-lashed gray eyes, till even Featherstone forgot his troubles in momentary admiration of her girlish beauty "Whatever I can do to save you without injustice to others I shall be glad to do."

"Flossy—no, I can never call you by that dear name again—Mrs.—Mrs. Kohala, do you mean that?" and Featherstone half lifted his hand as if expecting hers to meet it, then let it fall again.

"I do."

"Will you make me one promise?"

"What is it?"

"Say that you will make it; it will bring no harm to you. and it will help me."

"If such be the case I give you the promise," she said, with characteristic impulsiveness.

"It is that you do not repeat to any living soul what I have told you about Kohala till I remove the injunction of secrecy and silence."

"I will agree to that, on one condition."

"Name the condition."

"It is that you take me at once to Kohala."

"At once?"

"Yes, at once."

"But that would be ruin."

"How so?"

"I suppose you know that you and I are watched and followed by the spies of this fellow, Loring?"

"I do not care."

"But I do. Can you not wait till after one o'clock to-morrow night? Then, if you creep quietly out and keep in the shadows, you will find me awaiting you directly in front of the Mormon Church. I shall have a native guide along, who can take us so as to avoid the guards, and within an hour you will be with your husband. What say you?"

"I say yes; but if he were not a prisoner he would come to me. All the thrones in the world could not keep Kohala from me if he were free."

"I cannot explain all to you now. But it is understood that, till you see me again, you do not tell a soul what has passed between us; and, in the next place, that you will meet me at the hour named in front of the Mormon Church, which, you know, is only a short distance away. You may remember you were curious to hear the service, and I took you there one night?"

Marguerite nodded, and after fully a minute's hesitation, as if he were debating whether to say anything further or not, Featherstone bowed stiffly and left the house.

Kohala owned a fine house in Honolulu, and here he and Featherstone lived together since he returned from abroad; there were good servants and an excellent stable attached to the establishment, and these the captain continued to enjoy during the absence of their owner.

After leaving Mrs. Holmes he went directly to this house, and his first act was to order in a bottle of brandy and some soda. He filled a goblet with a great deal of the former and very little of the latter, and drained it off without taking it from his lips. Then he lit a cigar, poured out some more brandy so as to have it within reach, dropped into a dining-room chair and shot out a string of oaths, intended, no doubt, to relieve his over-wrought feelings.

As the reader must have already surmised, with the reasons for the same, it was Featherstone who caused Kohala to be abducted immediately in front of his wife's cottage, and conveyed in a closed carriage to a secluded house far up the long valley that leads to the Pali's bloody cliffs, some eight miles from Honolulu.

Featherstone did not appear directly in this enter-prise; he was far too shrewd for that; and tools suitable for his purpose, both white and brown, could be had at the lowest market rates for any such work as that.

Featherstone's plan was really very adroit. He pro-posed, with Marguerite to help him, to play the part of a brave liberator. But before he permitted—or, rather, Marguerite permitted—Kohala to return to Honolulu, Kohala, for her sake, would be induced to issue his pro-nunciamento, declaring himself King of Hawaii.

All this was now relegated to the impossibilities, and the all-important and difficult question presented to Featherstone's mind was how to save himself when the inevitable exposure came.

He smoked with such energy that he sat amid a cloud. He was a man fertile in resources, and no tenderness of conscience ever barred him from a scheme that prom-ised success by illegal methods.

The woman had deceived him, and he cursed her for it. It would have gladdened his savage heart to see her dead at his feet.

He reasoned that she would keep her promise of si-lence, and that she would meet him, as agreed. What if she and Kohala were never seen again? People would say they had eloped in some strange way. What if their dead bodies were found together, with an empty pistol clutched in Kohala's hand? People would say it was the romantic and insane end of two foolish lovers.

CHAPTER XX.

BLAKE GETS ON THE TRAIL.

FOR prudential reasons, Colonel Ellis and others who had a tender interest in the fate of Kohala, kept from the knowledge of the public the fact that he was missing; and the two daily papers, though fully appreciating the importance, as a matter of news, of the death, abduction or desertion of the young man, made no allusion to him in their columns.

The men whom Blake assigned to search the different sections of the city he had mapped out reported to him, one by one, each being forced to confess that his mission had been a failure, for the missing man had left no more sign than if the earth had opened in the darkness and swallowed him up, leaving no scar as a reminder on its surface.

This goes to prove how careful and complete had been Featherstone's plans. Indeed, Blake's suspicions as to this man's connection with the matter were the result of intuition rather than of reason.

After he had lost all hope of finding Kohala by means of the search he had instituted Blake sought out Colonel Ellis and said:

"I am going to let all the men go back to their commands and take up this matter by myself."

"But what are you going to do?" asked Colonel Ellis, whose anxiety for the safety of Kohala had preyed on him more than all the cares of the revolution and the burdens that followed it.

"I want Colonel Loring"—Loring was present—"to give me a leave of absence for as long as I may want it."

"I shall write it out now," said Colonel Loring, and he pulled up to the table and dashed off the following:

' HEADQUARTERS PROVISIONAL ARMY OF HAWAII:

To whom it may concern—The bearer, First Lieutenant Harry Blake, is detailed for special service by me, and all officers and enlisted men connected with this command are hereby instructed to assist Lieutenant Blake in such manner as he may require or request.

"ARTHUR LORING, Colonel Commanding."

"I don't think I shall call upon my comrades for much help," said Blake, as he folded up the paper and put it away in his ample breast-pocket. "This is to be a still hunt. One doesn't go gunning for wild ducks with a brass band, as we used to say in the States."

After leaving headquarters Blake went to a public-house down near the pier of the Union Steamship Company, and here, in a back room, he found Phipps, sober, or, rather, comparatively so, for he was in that taciturn state of inebriety when he might be said to be at his best.

Phipps, for State reasons and not because he had any fondness for the woman, had been very attentive to Clem of late, and it was through him and in consideration of Colonel Ellis's bribes, that she was induced to tell all she knew about her mistress and to adorn her facts through her imagination, in order to give what she considered full measure for value received.

"Phipps," said Blake, as he handed the Irishman a cigar and lit another himself, "I want you to help me."

"I'm ready," said Phipps.

"You know Mrs. Clem?"

"Faith, I do."

"And you don't love her?"

"Love her!"

"Yes."

"Do I look like a natoral born fool?"

"Far from it, Phipps."

"Then don't insult a man of my taste."

"But you've been sweet on her."

"Mebby so; but be the same token, I'd be sweet on Owld Nick's grandmother, if it would only help to annex these islands to the great United States," said Phipps, with energy.

"I think you told me that this Mrs. Clem is attached to Featherstone?"

"And, sure, she should be; doesn't he pay her for it?"
"How much does he pay her?"
"I don't know. But why do you ask?"
"Because Featherstone called on Mrs. Holmes to-day,
and if it was possible, you may depend on it that Mrs.
Clem overheard their conversation, and that they spoke
about the man we want to find."
"Ah, be gob, I see!" said Phipps, closing one eye.
"I was sure you would. Now, it is near dark, and you
can find Mrs. Clem and have a private chat with her
without exciting attention. Go to her as soon as you
can and learn everything you can about this meeting
and report it to me at this place at nine o'clock. If
you need money let me know, and you can have all
you want."
"I'll keep an account of ixpenses, but I have all I want
for the present," said Phipps, and, full of his purpose,
he started off, for it was now dusk, and the lamps and
electric lights were burning as brightly as in the happiest days of Honolulu.
Promptly at nine o'clock Phipps returned and made
his way to the little back room where he last saw Blake.
The only occupant of the place now was a native fisher-
man, dressed in a blouse and straw hat and loose cotton
trousers, and with the long black hair and smooth brown
face that distinguish his class.
"Faith, I thought I'd be afther seein' Mr. Blake here,"
said Phipps, as, with a disgusted look at the Kanaka, he
was about to retreat.
"Mr. Blake is here."
Phipps started. It could not be that brown man with
the half-closed eyes who had so perfectly imitated the
voice of his friend.
"Did you spake to me?" he said, addressing himself
to the native.
"I did." And then, with a dumb laugh, Blake—for
he it was—rose and gave Phipps his hand.
"Well, begorra, you take the cake!" said Phipps, step-
ping back and examining the disguise with intense admiration and many strong but unquotable expressions
of surprise. "Sure, your own mother wouldn't know

you if she was to clap her two eyes on you this blessed minute."

"If any one else should come in, Phipps, or if you should chance to see me on the street in this disguise, you must not know me."

"No, not from a side of sole leather."

"And now tell me what you have done," said Blake, sinking his voice to the pitch he wanted the other to imitate.

"I didn't larn much, for Mrs. Clem was as close as a clam. Featherstone owns her, body and soul. She said him and the little woman had a row to-day, and that it isn't over by a long shot. And, after much coaxin', she gave me her word of honor as a lady—just think of that, Mr. Blake!—that she believed the young gentleman we are so anxious to find is alive and well."

"How did she learn that?"

"She didn't say."

"It was not from her mistress?"

"No. I'm most sure of that."

"Then, Phipps, she must have overheard Featherstone saying so."

"That's my belief."

"Good; you have found out all I want to know. If you could get Clem to drink a little wine to-night she might be more communicative; suppose you try it, Phipps."

"All right, Mr. Blake; and may you have the same good luck as a Kanaka that you always had as a white man," and, with this, the two men shook hands and parted.

Blake was so confident of his disguise that he took no pains to keep in the shadows, but sauntered through the streets with the inevitable cheroot between his lips, and evidently indifferent to the eager groups discussing the situation before the bars.

He passed the building where the sailors from the American warship were quartered, and he watched with some interest a man fastening, over the circular arch of the gateway leading into the grounds, a signboard, on which, in gold and black letters, was the legend: "CAMP BOSTON."

Not an arrow-shot away was Kohala's house, in which he knew Featherstone still lived. Although it was a warm night the shutters were closed and the curtains were drawn; but they did not entirely conceal the glow that told there was a light on the other side, with some one to enjoy it.

Blake knew that the servants here were all men and natives and that they were devoted to Kohala, for they had been brought over to wait on him from his plantation in Hawaii after his return from abroad. But as they were a single-minded lot, and could have been easily influenced by Featherstone, he thought it ad_visable not to communicate with them directly.

He went back to the stable, directed thither by the low hum of voices, and he succeeded in secreting himself so as to be able to overhear all that was being said without attracting attention.

Blake was interested to learn that the subject uppermost in his mind was the one that agitated the men at the stable. In hushed and almost tearful voices they discussed the absence of their master, and one of them, evidently voicing the sentiments of his companions, said:

"If our master does not come back in two more suns I shall run off and make my way home to my wife in Hawaii. I do not like this white man, and my heart would be lighter if he was away and Kohala was here."

"This was said in the Hawaiian tongue, otherwise Featherstone, who had advanced from the house through the darkness without being seen and with as little noise as if he were a shadow, must have heard this opinion of himself.

Addressing the group of men, who huddled together as if frightened as soon as they became aware of his presence, Featherstone said:

"I am going away, and may not be back till near daylight. Do you hear me, Kam?"

"Ye—yes, sa, I heah yo'," said one of the men, with

an accent very much like that of a plantation negro in the Cotton States.

Kam was Kohala's major-domo, a big, gentle, single-hearted fellow, who, till the return of his young master, had never been off the great sugar plantation on Hawaii since he was born there, thirty-five years before.

"And, Kam?"

"Yes, sa."

"Don't leave the house."

"Oh, no, sa; I no leave."

"And if any one calls and asks for me you tell them I am asleep and feeling very sick. Do you understand that, Kam?"

"Oh, yes, sa; I on'stan'," said the man.

Blake, who was crouching close up against the stable wall, expected to hear Featherstone saying something that would indicate his departure, but he could not catch even the fall of his feet. He had evidently gone as quickly and mysteriously as he had come, and the natives must have known it, for they resumed their low-voiced use of their liquid, full-voweled mother tongue.

Featherstone had gone, not back to the house certainly, but in what direction Blake was, for the instant, at a loss to determine.

Again that peculiar intuition, that does not come through reasoning, but which, no matter how manifested, is genius, came to Blake's help. With a sense as fine and acute as the bloodhound's, and which led him, instead of his directing it, he sprang lightly and noiselessly over the hedge and into the street. Without an instant's hesitation he turned his back to the city's lights and started out the street that led to the Punch Bowl, or which, for some distance, might be taken by those walking or driving to the great Pali Cliff.

There was nothing ahead, nothing behind him, nothing in sight to impel him to this course, yet he was as sure of his ground as if the midday sun were blazing down on the form of Featherstone a few paces in the advance.

Blake knew that Featherstone, like most Englishmen,

was an excellent pedestrian, and that once he was outside the city's limits and where there was no necessity
for care he would walk with great rapidity; but in
that the man on his trail was quite his equal, in addition to having superior powers of endurance.

It did not take Blake long to leave the city behind
him, and a silent, deserted road in front. Here and
there, to the right and left, he could see a light in the
little frame house of a Portuguese gardener, that indus-
trious and thrifty people owning and cultivating much
of the land on either side of the road along which he
sped.

He wore felt shoes that were even more noiseless in
their fall than the bare feet would have been. Now and
then Blake stopped to listen, sometimes placing his ear
to the ground, like an Indian on the trail who knows
that the solid earth is a better conductor of sound than
the air.

After each examination Blake hurried on with increased speed, which was an assurance of his increasing
confidence.

At length, and after having gone over a distance at
least two miles from the city's limit, he slackened his
pace and advanced with greater caution.

It was a clear, starlit night, and the air was as still
as if it had gone to sleep, so that even the droning of
an occasional beetle or the whiz of a passing bat made
a loud and disturbing noise.

The pawing and impatient snorting of horses at a halt
at length brought Blake's cautious advance to a stop.

He was about to move on again in the direction of the
animals—they might have strayed into the highway from
their pastures—when he heard the penetrating, sibilant
whispering of men in front.

Down on hands and knees he dropped and crept rapidly
forward till he was within twenty feet of the men, whose
dark forms could be seen against the stars as they stood
beside their horses.

"Very well, Pedro, we can discuss this as we go on.
Mount, my man, for there is no time to lose."

Blake recognized Featherstone's voice. From the name

"Pedro" he inferred that the other man was a Portuguese. He had just reached this conclusion, and was deploring the fact that he was on foot, when the two men sprang into their saddles with the ease of skilled horsemen and galloped away in the direction of the Pali.

CHAPTER XXI.

KOHALA'S SITUATION.

THE plan to kidnap Kohala was not made on the spur of the moment. For a long time Featherstone had thought of it as an alternative to which he might be forced in the event of the Americans deposing the Queen.

Through his emissaries, the night of the revolution, he kept track of the young man from the time he went to the rendezvous where the troops under Colonel Loring assembled up to the minute that he was sent with the message to Colonel Ellis at the Hawaiian Hotel.

The looked-for opportunity came just when Kohala, disappointed at not finding Marguerite Holmes at home, left the cottage and turned into the dark street encumbered with the building material of the new Episcopal church, which prevented its being a thoroughfare at night.

Featherstone had a closed carriage in waiting, and he was inside the carriage when two masked men, with pistols in their right hands, forced Kohala inside.

Featherstone was playing the part of prisoner. He had been seized in the same way, so he told Kohala, and what the outcome of it was to be he did not know; but he was sure that the Americans were at the bottom of the outrage and that he was made a victim because he was the friend of Kohala, whom they wanted to get out of the way so that there might be no obstacle to their scheme of annexation.

"But," said Featherstone, as the carriage, with the blinds pulled down, sped out of the illuminated streets and into the dark country, "I have always been ready to lay down my life for you, and if it comes to that now I shall not flinch from the sacrifice; all I ask is that they save yourself so that some day you may inherit your rights."

Kohala believed this implicitly, and more worldly men, finding themselves in the same position, would have shown the same credulity.

He believed that the captain was a prisoner, and he regretted it more than he did the danger that threatened himself, for his friend's suffering was because of his fidelity, and Kohala had a royal appreciation of this quality.

Of late he had not felt as warmly toward Featherstone as he did before their coming to Hawaii.

He did not like his monarchical tendencies; but, above all, he did not like the familiar way in which he spoke of Marguerite Holmes. But now, with youthful generosity, he chided himself for ever having harbored an unkind thought of this noble and devoted friend.

It should be said that as soon as Kohala was seized his pistol was taken from him, and he was threatened with instant death if he made an outcry or attempted to escape. Featherstone had the same story to tell, and he gave it as his opinion that the purpose of their captors was to hold them for a ransom.

"Though," he said, with his mouth close to Kohala's ear as the carriage rolled on, "it may be that these men are your warmest adherents, and that their purpose is to get you away from the influence of the Americans and make you King of Hawaii in spite of yourself."

To this Kohala made no response. He knew that the men who made him prisoner were Portuguese, and he believed that the Queen's party were responsible for the outrage.

After two hours' rapid driving the road became so rough that the horses were brought down to a walk, and then Kohala learned, from the sounds behind, that they were being followed by two mounted men.

The beating of branches against the carriage roof and the crashing under the wheels and the horses' feet told that they were going through a dense underbrush and over a route that had not been much traveled.

It was to Kohala, who was consumed by curiosity rather than fear, as if the sun had gone down for the last time. It seemed an age since he had parted from Colonel Ellis and a year of black torture since he had entered this jolting vehicle.

At length the carriage halted, and the barking of a pack of curs told that they were in the neighborhood of a house, a fact that was soon confirmed by the flashing of lights and the stamping of many feet on a wide piazza.

A man with a perforated tin lantern came to the carriage door, and, pulling it open, he said, with a foreign accent:

"This is the place, gentlemen; get out."

They were conducted into the house, which, though in a state of decay, looked as if it had at one time been a place of some pretensions.

"Now, gentlemen," said the man with the lantern, "I can assure you both that if you remain quiet and make no attempt to get away you will be kindly treated. We must keep you in separate rooms, and you need not be afraid of sleeping till you are entirely rested."

"May I ask why you have brought us here?" asked Kohala.

"You are free to ask any questions you choose; but to-night, at least, you will get no answers," said the man with the lantern.

Kohala was conducted to a bedroom in a wing of the building; but as he shook hands with Featherstone, who saw fit to affect depression, he whispered to him:

"Do not lose heart, captain; depend on it, our friends will be sure to find us and all will be well again."

As soon as Kohala had been taken out of sight and hearing Featherstone burst into a fit of laughter, and, grasping the hand of the man who had been officiating with the lantern, he said:

"Well, Pedro, old man, that worked like a charm. Never saw anything neater since I was born. Come, let us celebrate the event with a stiff glass of brandy, and be quick about it, for I must be home and in my little bed before daylight."

"Pedro was evidently the master of the establishment and the father of the pretty dark-eyed girl who brought in the brandy and water, and whom Featherstone tried to compliment by saying she was fit to be the wife of a king, and adding:

"And who knows but you may be a queen yet, sweet Annetta."

The girl laughed and showed her white teeth in a way that told her delight with the flattery. She evidently knew that her father and Featherstone wished to be alone, for as soon as she had set the liquor and glasses before them she bowed and withdrew.

"Now, Pedro," said Featherstone, after they had drained their glasses and he had risen and was buttoning up his coat, "remember we are playing for big stakes."

"Trust me not to forget," said Pedro, with a knowing shake of the bushy, black head and an uninviting exhibition of tobacco-stained teeth.

"Take good care of our young friend and see that he does not get out of your sight. Of course, he will want to know why he is held here, and, of course, you will impress on him the fact that you are acting under orders and that it is for his own good and safety."

"Oh, I understand all that. If there's any mistake, captain, it won't be through me. I don't swear and bluster like you English and Americans, but I think and I act," and Pedro tapped his forehead and winked one eye to show that he thought himself quite as quick and clever as he did the man advising him.

With a perfect understanding as to what was to be done in the case of expected and unexpected emergencies Featherstone went out to the carriage in which he and Kohala had come and was driven back to the city.

The bedroom in which Kohala found himself was, or, . rather, had been, elaborately furnished. But the great four-poster bed, with its yellow canopy and torn mosquito netting, the chairs with the upholstery stained and ragged, the heavy curtains that suggested insect flights and dust clouds if they were touched, and the floor, covered with faded Turkish rugs, all bespoke a day of luxury, if not of taste, that had long since departed. Kohala was something of a fatalist; perhaps it would describe him more accurately to say he was a philosopher. He realized that he was tired, and that neither fretting nor personal effort could better his situation, so he wisely took of his coat and boots, extinguished the light and threw himself on the bed.

It was an occasion, if ever one had come in his life, when he could not fairly be charged with selfishness if he gave all his thoughts to the situation in which he was placed and the dangers that unquestionably threatened him; but instead, he thought of Marguerite, the wife whom he had not seen since the hour when they were married, and he, with his joyous secret locked close in his heart, started off to visit the woman to whom he had been betrothed without his own consent.

As he thought it over he became more and more convinced that he had done an unwise thing in keeping his secret from Colonel Ellis; but never, from first to last, did he regret the act that made the woman he loved his wife. Had it not been for his capture he would have told Colonel Ellis what he had done the morning following the revolution, and if the colonel and others objected, as he expected they would do, he was resolved to sell out his property and take his wife to any country she preferred, for no matter where it might be between the Equator and the Poles he felt he would be happy with her.

All his love for Hawaii, and his readiness to aid her through any sacrifice but one, remained. In one thing, his marriage, in which he was himself the most profoundly interested, he could not, as a free man, permit others to interfere; and who will say that he was not right?

From thoughts of Marguerite he gradually drifted off into dreams of her, and sleep accomplished what would have been impossible to him if awake, for it brought her to his side.

When he awoke the sun was shining in through the faded curtains, and an old, wrinkled woman, Pedro's mother, was moving about the room like a sprightly, light-footed ghost that by some means had got into the wrong body.

As soon as the old woman saw that the young man was awake she darted out of the room, as if alarmed at the sight; but in less than a minute she was back again with a little plaited tray on which was a cup of coffee and some crackers.

"Eat some, then you feel good." Having said this, the old woman sat down the tray and again darted out.

Kohala dressed, by putting on his coat and pulling on his boots. then he went to one of the two windows, and, pushing back the faded curtains, looked out.

The prospect was not inviting. A high hill shut out the view a few hundred yards away. A few scraggy palms, towering over a great expanse of that curse of the islands, yellow lantana, looked as if they had strayed up from the shore and were hopelessly lost. There were lemon and orange trees, sadly in need of pruning, near the house, and some sickly decorative plants and flowers that looked as if they had grown weary of the struggle for existence under the most depressing difficulties.

He saw a number of lean yellow curs and draggle-tailed chickens scurrying through the weeds, and he heard in the distance the neighing of a horse.

He was about to let the curtains fall and turn back to the coffee when two villainous-looking men, with heavy black beards and long black hair, came to view, and, as they halted for consultation under a palm, one of them drew a long knife from his belt and gave an outlet to his energy by slashing into the bark.

CHAPTER XXII.

A PLACE OF MANY MYSTERIES.

THE man who never knows fear cannot be truthfully called a brave man. He only is brave who, despite his

fear of the danger, resolutely dares to face it. The sight
of the man under the palm was not calculated to allay the
suspicions of Kohala as to the difficulties that environed
him; yet, even when he saw that the men noticed him
and moved away, as if annoyed at their discovery, his
color did not change nor did his heart beat faster.

When the men had disappeared in the jungle of underbrush Kohala stepped back and drank his coffee and ate
the crackers without any sign of agitation.

He found appliances for washing and combing his hair,
though they were newer and cheaper, and so not in
keeping with the furnishings of the dingy old apartment.

He had finished brushing his wavy black hair when
he heard a rap at the door, and, before he could speak
the "come in" that rose to his lips, it was opened, and
Annetta, looking like a bacchante, with a wreath of
crimson flowers about her blue-black hair, entered, and,
with a blush that added to the healthy beauty of her
face and a bow that told she was not versed in that
manner of salutation, she said:

"May it please Your Majesty, breakfast is ready."

"Majesty!" repeated Kohala, with amused surprise,
"why, my young friend, I am not a king."

"No, sir," said Annetta, with more confidence, "but
you can be one whenever you say the word, and that's
the same thing."

"It may be—and then it may not; but we will let that
pass. What is your name?"

"Annetta."

"Annetta what?"

"Just Annetta, if Your Majesty pleases."

"Have you a father?"

"Oh, yes, sir."

"What is his name?"

"Pedro, may it please you."

"Pedro what?"

"That is all, sir."

"No surname?"

"I do not know what that is."

"What is your nationality?"

"I do not know."

"Where were you born?"

"In Honolulu."

"And your father?"

"He is a Portuguese."

"What is the name of this place?'

"May it please Your Majesty, it has none."

"Upon my word," said Kohala, with a laugh that
seemed to fascinate the girl, "you appear to have a
mysterious dearth of names here. But you said something about breakfast."

"Yes. Your Majesty."

"Why do you call me 'Your Majesty'?"

"Because I was told to do so."

"By whom?"

"My father."

"Does he own this place?"

"I do not know."

"Is he here?"

"No, sir."

"Where is he?"

"I do not know."

"Well, Annetta, I shall not try further to exhaust your
information, though I am sorry to see it is sadly limited
in the directions that most interest me."

The girl had evidently been instructed as to what she
must do and say, for she held the door open for Kohala
to pass out, and, as soon as he had done so, she darted
ahead and led him into a little apartment that showed
signs of having been recently fitted up as a private dining-room.

He found the table set for one. He expected to see
Featherstone, for the true state of affairs never dawned
on him, and as he was not there, he asked Annetta the
reason, and was answered by a shrug of the shoulders
and the same "I do not know, sir."

Kohala made no further investigations. The breakfast was ample, varied and well-cooked and served,
Annetta being the only person he saw during the meal.

As soon as he had finished breakfast his pretty attendant, who seemed delighted to be able to wait on him,

led him into still another apartment off the dining-room, and said:

"This is Your Majesty's parlor, and you will find good cigars on the table, and there is wine over in that closet, and some books in the one near it, if Your Maj esty cares to read. And if you should want anything further please to ring this little bell and I shall come to you, for I will be in waiting in the next room and anxious to serve you."

Having delivered herself of this little speech, which sounded as if she had repeated it over before and was not quite certain of the part, Annetta bowed again, blushed becomingly and was about to leave, when Kohala called to her:

"Wait a moment. Annetta."

"Yes, Your Majesty," and she turned and bowed, as if that, too, were something she had been instructed not to forget in her intercourse with the young man.

"You treat me as if I were a prince."

"And so you are, Your Majesty."

"Then I must be a free man and so at liberty to walk about these grounds as I choose." Seeing that she looked doubting and confused, he added: "But perhaps I am a prisoner? If so, I have no fault to find with my jailer, though I can't say so much for my captors."

Annetta did not understand his compliment, but she never lost sight of the part that had been assigned her.

"If Your Majesty pleases," she said, "it will be better that you should remain in the house."

"In what way better?"

"It will be safer."

"Then there is danger outside?"

"Yes, Your Majesty."

"Guards?"

"Oh, yes, but—"

"But what, Annetta? Speak out."

"If Your Majesty were to go outside and any harm were to come to you the blame would fall on me."

"Who would blame you?"

"I cannot tell you names."

"Very well. Can you tell me where the gentleman is

who was brought here a prisoner with me last night?"
"I cannot."
"You are ordered not to: is that it?"
"Yes, Your Majesty."
"But you can tell me, surely, if he is living and well?"
"He is living and well, Your Majesty," and fearing
to say more, if, indeed, she had not already said too
much, Annetta left the room.

Kohala lit a cigar—it was a good one—and feeling
that the only wise course left him was to remain quiet
and await developments, he got a book out of the closet
and threw himself on the sofa. His getting the book
was the result of habit, for he never looked into it, but
laid it on his breast, closed his eyes, and, with his fingers
interlocked about his head, he gave free rein to his specu-
lations.

Now and then he rose and took a turn about the room,
or looked out through the grimy windows at the dreary
prospect outside; but he never did so without seeing the
two men whom he first noticed under the palm that
morning.

The fact that the men who took his pistol from him
the night before left him his wallet and watch convinced
him that they were not ordinary robbers, though he did
not lose sight of the fact that it was in their power to get
possession of these articles any time they wanted them.

His watch had never been such company nor had he
ever consulted it so often before in the same space of
time. He was looking at its face and saw it was one
o'clock when Annetta again came in to tell him that
luncheon awaited him in the adjoining room.

"You are very kind, Annetta," he said; "but I am
sorry to have troubled you, for I do not feel at all
hungry."

"Is Your Majesty ill?" she asked, with unaffected
anxiety.

"Could you expect any man to feel well in my position,
Annetta? Would you feel well and happy if you were
in my place?"

Her lips trembled and she hesitated, then she said,
though it evidently was not what she had intended saying:

"If you will not go to luncheon, then there are some men who would like to speak with Your Majesty."

"Who are they?"

"They are your friends, but I cannot tell their names."

"Very well, Annetta, in Heaven's name show them in, and if there is any 'worst' to this thing they may be able to tell me what it is."

Annetta went to the door, whispered to some one outside, then the cracked voice of the old woman was heard calling to a third party, in a language Kohala did not understand, and this was followed by the tramping of heavily shod feet on a bare wooden floor.

The tramping came nearer, and Kohala looked up to see five men entering the room, with Pedro, whom he recognized as the man who had carried the lantern, at their head. The young man noticed, further, that his visitors all had big black beards of exactly the same cut, and as these appendages did not match their hair and faces, he came to the conclusion that they were assumed for the purpose of disguise.

Kohala rose, and his visitors respectfully stood before him in line, with their eyes fixed humbly on the hats which they held in their hands.

"Your Majesty," began Pedro, "we are all your true, good friends, and we've come here to talk with you and to tell you that it's because we love you that we took you away last night from people—from the Americans—that we know are your enemies."

"I suppose I should feel very grateful to you for this extremely thoughtful precaution," said Kohala, his sarcasm entirely wasted on the men before him, "and particularly in showing me that the people I have been regarding as friends are, in truth, my enemies. Of course, you have informed the Americans that you brought me here and why you did it?"

Not at all abashed by this, Pedro replied:

"No, we haven't; there'll be plenty of time to act when Your Majesty gives the word."

"But I am not a majesty," said Kohala, with less patience than he had shown to Annetta when she addressed him in the same way.

"No; but you will be a king as soon as you say the word, and that's why we are here," said Pedro, with the confident manner of a man sure of his ground.

"But whom do you represent?"

•"We represent the foreign element on these islands; and outside, waiting to see Your Majesty, are a score of Hawaiians, who represent a large majority of all the natives."

"And what is your purpose and theirs?"

"We want you to proclaim your rights."

"What do you mean?"

"We know, and Your Majesty knows, you are the rightful sovereign of Hawaii. You may not want to be king, but the people want it, and you owe it to them to speak out."

"I might as well have it over with both parties at once," said Kohala. "Show my countrymen in."

"Before doing that, Your Majesty, and before making up your mind, which it's necessary to be careful about, it is right that I should tell you that if you refuse the wishes of these people who are so ready to lay down their lives for you, that they may come to look on you as a traitor to their cause, and then I would not want to be responsible for what they may do," said Pedro.

There was no misunderstanding this. It presented the case to Kohala in an entirely new, and by no means an alluring, aspect.

Whether the men in the room or the natives waiting outside represented the elements they claimed to or no, Kohala felt that they were desperate—his own capture warranted that belief—and that if he did not comply or seem to comply with their demands he might be disposed of, as had one of his ancestors a few generations back.

He had sufficient self-command to conceal his nervousness and the quickness of thought that under such circumstances is a mark of true greatness.

"Show in my countrymen," he said, "and let us talk like friends."

CHAPTER XXIII.

A TRYING SITUATION.

.ALTHOUGH he had seen much of the world in a geo-graphical sense, Kohala was a child in his judgment of men, and, like all guileless and impulsive natures, he was influenced by exteriors and inclined to believe that all men—at least, those to whom he gave his esteem—were as honest and truthful as himself.

He saw, or thought he saw, the reason for his being abducted from Honolulu, and so, while he could not reconcile himself to the treatment, he regarded it with less indignation when he came to think that it was done for what these devoted but mistaken people thought to be for his own good.

Not so much to avert the danger that might threaten himself as to save his friends from excesses that might result in their own ruin, Kohala made up his mind not to oppose them; but at the same time not to commit himself to a course which, if followed out on the lines of its initiation, would defeat its own purpose.

He could not know that Pedro and his countrymen, entirely indifferent to the form of government in Hawaii, were working for the reward which, in addition to a guarantee, Featherstone was to pay them in the event of success.

Delighted and surprised at Kohala's frankness, Pedro suggested that they adjourn to the large dining-room where there would be space for the whole party to assemble.

This being agreed to, Kohala was escorted to a larger room near by, the antique furniture of which told of better and cleaner days. Annetta escorted in the natives, not one of whom Kohala could recall having ever seen before; but they looked to be respectable, earnest men, and they saluted him, as was the custom of old in salut-ing a king, by touching their right hands to the ground and then laying them on their bowed heads.

Kohala was given a large chair at the head of the

table, and, as there were not chairs enough, the others stood up in a line about the wall.

The silence that followed was becoming embarrassing when Pedro, who stood at the foot of the table, and who, as proprietor of the place, if not from his belief in his own superior intelligence, appointed himself master of ceremonies, said, for the benefit of the newcomers:

"I have told Kohala of Hawaii that, as we have no longer a queen and do not want the Americans to rule us, that we now regard him as our king, quite as much as if we saw him seated on the throne established by his great ancestor, Kamehameha, in Honolulu."

The black eyes of the natives took in fire while Pedro was speaking, and at the conclusion they threw up their arms like one man and shouted till the old rafters rang with the echoes:

"Long live Kohala of Hawaii!"

A tall native with iron-gray hair, an erect figure and a scar across his bronzed brow that added to his military aspect, advanced to the foot of the table, and, after bowing very low to Kohala, cast a quick glance at his companions, as if to invoke their attention, and said, with the voice and manner of a natural born orator:

"Last night messengers from Keona of Hawaii came to this island of Oahu to get the voice of the people and to learn how many of us were ready to renounce Queen Liliuokalani and to give allegiance to Kohala. I speak only for those whom I know, and in my sixty years of life, during which our people have dwindled to one-half, I think I can say I know all the living and remember the many dead of those many seasons.

"The Queen is of our race, yet she shows her contempt for us by marrying Dominis, a white man, and, except the few who feed on her crumbs, we do not like her; and now that she is down, we rejoice in her fall, though no native hand was raised to bring it about, and we can never submit to the rule of the white men who have dethroned her.

"I remember the day when Kohala was born in Hawaii, for I was then in the employ, as a herdsman, of the great chief, his father. There was much rejoicing

among the people on the pastures and on the plantations that day, and they said, one to the other: 'Courage, for the child is born who will yet save us, and, from
the throne of the great Conqueror, make us happy.'

"I recall the night, in the sacred cavern up by the
lake of fire, when Kohala of Hawaii was betrothed to
the little daughter of the chief Keona. When the sun
rose in the morning it saw us feasting by the sea, and
the maidens danced and sang about the flower bowers
where slept the children on whom our future depended.

"Since that day we have watched and prayed for Kohala. We did not like it when, as a boy, he went beyond the great world of waters from which the sun
rises; but we became reconciled when we reasoned that
there lay the land of the white man and that there our
prince would learn the ways that have made the white
man our master and use them so that we should become,
at least, his equal.

"Since Kohala's return there has come to us the story
that he, too, would wed among the whites; but we did
not, we could not believe it, for we knew his race and
that the son would die ere he broke the pledge of the
father.

"And now we have come to council with our prince,
who needs but to say the word and he will be our king.
Swift runners await within call to spread the news of
his declaration through Oahu, and boats with lowered
sails await the messengers who are to carry the glad
tidings to our sister islands. If we would succeed
there is no time to lose. A minute's hesitation may
be fatal. What says Kohala of Hawaii?"

There was no mistaking this man's earnestness, and
had he made no allusion to marriage Kohala might have
been more thrilled by the patriotic fervor of his adherent.

But he had taken a step which he would not retrace
if he could. He had deliberately turned his back on a
throne, for which he did not care, to be the husband of
a woman who was more to him than all else in life.

Had he obeyed the impulse that came on him with a
force that it cost a powerful effort to resist he would
have told the old orator and his friends, then and there,

that he did not want to be the king of Hawaii; and, further, that he had, as a man, ignored the pledge made for him by his father when he was a child; but he felt that if he were to do so the men who were ready to worship him as the possible savior of their country would, in their wild fury at the discovery, destroy him as a traitor. That he had the tact that is often more potent than valor was shown by his reply. He determined not to refer to his marriage, nor to the fact that he regarded himself as a prisoner, but to show that the action of Keona in getting the voice of the people as to their choice of a ruler showed that a new and better method of selecting sovereigns had come to Hawaii.

But, adroit though this was, it did not satisfy Pedro or the natives. They wanted Kohala to at once claim the throne by proclamation, as the only way of getting it at all.

"No," said Kohala, his patience at length threatening to give way, "I can make no proclamation from this place. Here I am virtually a prisoner. I am not blind to this fact, though you treat me as a king. I will not say that you are not all entirely honest in your purpose; but if I am fit to rule when king my opinions should have weight while I am a private citizen. I see you agree to that. Very well, when I am assured that a majority of the people in these islands want me then I shall act, but not before. That is my answer, and it is folly longer to take up your time in discussion."

The men looked at each other in a disappointed way. True, Kohala had not absolutely rejected their advice, but he had not accepted it, as they thought he would. The more impulsive of the natives had been talking of a war under the lead of the young king, and so those who heard him were inclined to think that his caution was cowardice, and that contact with the whites had made him effeminate.

The impression that he was still a prisoner was verified when Pedro and two of his countrymen escorted him back to the little sitting-room assigned him by Annetta that morning, and where he was told he must "please remain for the present."

The natives lived near by in the Nuuanu Valley, where their thatched huts were set amid plantations of bananas.

At the head of this valley, and only two miles away, though Kohala had only the vaguest idea of his whereabouts, there was the appalling precipice of the Pali, with the fair heights of Lanihuli smiling down on the scene of Kamehameha's last battle for united Hawaii.

When night come Kohala was permitted to take a walk, accompanied by Pedro, who, in his earnestness to earn the reward offered by Featherstone, tried again to impress the young man with the necessity for issuing a proclamation at once. And on his part, Kohala, still loyal to the man he thought his friend, sought in vain to learn what had become of the captain. The only assurance he could get, and that was far from convincing, was that the Englishman was safe and that he had gone away that morning with the natives to try and direct matters to his—Kohala's—advantage.

Annetta, evidently infatuated with her father's detained guest, did everything in her power to make him comfortable, and she showed an inclination to remain talking with him that might have flattered him had not her purpose to impress him favorably brought more vividly before him the sweet face of the wife from whom he had been parted at the altar.

Driven to desperation by the danger and uncertainty of his situation Kohala made up his mind to make one effort for freedom that night.

Apart from removing his boots he did not undress, but threw himself on the bed, determined to get out through the window after midnight.

Despite his efforts to keep awake he dropped off to sleep. He was aroused by the tramping of heavy feet, and, looking up, he saw by the flash of a lantern that Featherstone, with a look of indescribable hate in his face, was bending over him.

Kohala, who had been dreaming of escape, sprang from the bed, and the two men stood looking at each other, Featherstone being the first to speak:

"They let me go away to help you," he stammered, "and I have just got back."

"Got back from where?" asked Kohala, and he pulled on his boots and glanced up at his visitor, whose face looked livid in the light of the lantern, which he still held as high as his head, though the expression of hate had vanished from his bloodshot eyes.

"From Honolulu," said Featherstone, evidently surprised at the energetic manner of his young friend.

"And they let you go there?"

"They did."

"Then you told my friends of my situation?"

"No. I had to pledge myself to these people that I would not see Colonel Ellis. But I did see Mrs. Holmes."

"And how is she?" asked Kohala, eagerly.

"She seems to be well."

"And you told her I was here?"

"I did not."

"You did not?"

"No."

"May I ask the reason?"

"Because she had so much to tell of herself that she had no time to make inquiries after you," said Featherstone, and he set the lantern down and faced Kohala.

"The meeting does not seem to have sweetened your temper, Captain Featherstone," said Kohala, with dignity "But it strikes me as not a little strange that you, claiming to be my friend, have been given your liberty and that you have not used it to get me out of this place."

"Yes, Kohala, I have been your friend, and your true friend; but I have just learned that you are not worthy the confidence I have given you and the efforts I have made for your elevation."

"I certainly do not understand you, captain."

"Then I shall be plainer."

"I wish you would."

"Without saying one word to me about it, you got married."

"I certainly did not think your consent to my marriage at all essential to make it binding, nor do I think so now. May I ask who gave you the information?"

"The lady herself."

"My wife tells only the truth."

"Ha! are you sure she is your wife?"

"I am certain."

"And that she has not another husband living?"

"You dare not intimate as much to me," said Kohala, his eyes ablaze with indignation. "You insult me, when you dare to reflect on the integrity of the woman I have made my wife! But if she were what you intimate— and you know you lie in your throat when you say it— then you must have known it when you introduced me • and did all in your power to keep us together! Feather-stone, I am neither blind nor a fool. Much that has puzzled me seems clear as daylight now You need not frown. I do not fear you. Go!" and Kohala pointed imperiously to the door; and Featherstone, not daring to trust himself longer, for he was clutching at the stock of the pistol in his pocket, went out to consult with Pedro, who was awaiting him.

CHAPTER XXIV.

BLAKE UNDERSTANDS HUMAN NATURE.

NOT Richard himself, at Bosworth Field, wished for a horse more earnestly than did Blake, when, in the darkness, he heard Featherstone and his companion rid-ing away.

He knew that it would be folly to try to follow them on foot, so he stood still till the pounding of the horses' hoofs died out in the direction of the Nuuanu Valley, and from this he inferred that the young man he was in search of was concealed up in that direction.

Feeling that he had accomplished something, Blake made his way back to the city, and, like a prudent man who understood that his success depended on keeping up his strength, he found his own quarters and went to bed.

The next morning he called on Colonel Ellis and re-ported all that had happened the previous evening. On hearing that Featherstone was possibly responsible for

Kohala's abduction the colonel, who knew from the guards that the man had been seen coming into the city early that morning, was for arresting him at once. "I think that would defeat our plans, if, indeed, it did not result in the death of the man we are so anxious to save," said Blake. "If we seize Featherstone he will deny everything and appeal to the English Consul for protection. No, colonel, we must follow the fellow up and catch him red-handed. I think I see through his game, and if I am right, it is a bold and a deep one; but we can beat him at his own tricks. Just leave it to me."

At this point Colonel Loring came in, and when he heard Blake's story and suggestions he said :

"I am quite willing to trust Blake in this matter. I hope, however, that his confidence in himself will not lead him to attempt too much alone."

"No, colonel," said Blake, "if I find that help is needed I have your authority to get it, and depend on me to do so. I can tell you no more of my purpose, or, rather, of what I propose to do, for it may be modified by new conditions at any moment."

Blake was not a man of impulses, yet he confessed to his friend that some of his best work, when chief of police, had been done through unpremeditated acts. He left the Hawaiian Hotel, and so absorbed was he in what was uppermost in his mind that he gave no heed to the direction he was taking till he suddenly started, like one waking from a vivid dream, and found himself directly in front of the large cottage, a part of which he knew to be occupied by Marguerite Holmes.

He had often seen and admired the dainty little Englishwoman on the streets; but, as their lines of life lay wide apart, he had never spoken to her. Acting on the sudden impulse, he determined to do so now. "If no other good comes of it," he reasoned, as he made his way to the door, "I shall, at least, be able to tell whether it is Featherstone or Kohala who is the favored man."

Clem, looking more grim and prim than ever, answered Blake's ring, and in reply to his question if her mistress was in she asked, snappishly :

"Well, what if she is; who'll I say wants to see her?"

"Lieutenant Blake of the Provisional Army. I have no card."

The title had a soothing effect on Clem, for she unbent her face, if not her form, and strode rather than walked away, leaving Blake outside the closed door.

Presently she came back and said:

"Yes, sir; Mrs. Holmes is in, and she'll see you."

Blake was conducted into the sitting-room, and he was about to take a chair when Marguerite entered, looking very pretty and very pale, and with such an expression of helplessness in the long-lashed gray eyes as aroused the gallant fellow's sympathies at once.

"Mr. Blake, I believe; I am Mrs.—Mrs. Holmes," said Marguerite, and she waved him back to the chair from which he had risen.

Blake was not a vain man, and therefore was not given to pride himself on anything; but if he had been inclined to boast he might, with truth, have laid claims to a pretty thorough knowledge of what the world calls "human nature." He was favorably impressed by the slender little creature; her very helplessness appealing powerfully to his confidence, so he determined at once to be more direct than he ordinarily would have been.

"When you learn my mission, Mrs. Holmes," he said, "I am sure you will be quite ready to pardon what may seem to you like an intrusion."

"I can assure you," she said, with a bow and a sad little smile, "that I do not consider your presence an intrusion."

"Thanks. Now may I ask if you know Captain Featherstone?"

"Yes. I know him," she replied.

"He is a countryman of yours?"

"Yes, I believe he is English."

"How long have you known him?"

"I met him on the steamer, the *Monowai*, coming from San Francisco to Honolulu. Kohala was with him." There was a perceptible tremor in Marguerite's voice as she mentioned the dearly loved name.

"Ah, yes, Kohala!" exclaimed Blake, for that was the

subject he proposed leading up to, but she had saved him the trouble.

"Do you know anything of him? Tell me! Is there any news of him?"

There was that in the woman's voice and manner that told Blake the true situation quite as accurately as if she had taken him into her confidence and confessed her love.

"I am searching for Kohala now," said Blake, determined to come to the point at once. "You want to have him found?"

"Oh, God only knows how I do!" she cried, and she interlocked her fingers and compressed her lips as if to keep from breaking down.

"You can help me," he said.

"I?"

"Yes, you, madam, if you will."

"Then tell me how! Command me, and if it will help Kohala to have me walk the island on my hands and knees I am ready to do it. Why, sir, this thing has been killing me ever since I heard of it."

"Mrs. Holmes, you saw Featherstone late last night?"

"I did."

"And he spoke to you about Kohala?"

"He did."

"What did he say?"

"I—I cannot tell you."

"Why not, if you are so interested in the missing man?"

"I had to promise that I would not."

"Featherstone?"

"Yes."

"Then you do know where Kohala is?"

"If I did I should be with him. It is by keeping the secret that I can see him. But I must not break my pledge."

"An unwise pledge is better broken than kept. But you say you are to see Kohala?"

"That is promised me."

"And when is the promise to be kept?"

"To-night."

"At what hour?"

"It will be after midnight."

"And the man comes here?"

"No; I meet him."

"Where?"

"In front of the Mormon Church."

"Thanks. Now one more question, Mrs. Holmes."

"You can ask me a thousand. Oh, this doubt has distracted me!" she cried, with her hands pressed to her eyes.

"You do not admire Featherstone, then?"

"No; I loathe him."

"And yet you are willing to intrust yourself to his protection."

"What else can I do? I shall die if I do not see Kohala!" And in her excitement she rose and began to pace the room.

"I think," said Blake, speaking very slowly, as was his habit when he came to a conclusion, "that I see through the situation very clearly. When you are with Featherstone to-night—and I believe it will help if you can keep the appointment—I shall try to arrange matters so that aid will not be far off if you need it. But don't lose heart. When things are at their worst, they say, they begin to mend. I thank you for this interview, and if you wouldn't mind making another pledge I'd like you to promise me that you won't say anything to Featherstone about my coming here."

"I promise that from my heart; and I shall pray Heaven to prosper your brave efforts for me and mine," she said, as she gave Blake her hand when he rose to go.

As the door had been left open and this conversation was carried on in low tones Clem, who had passed and repassed in the hope of being able to overhear something that might be sold to advantage, was grievously disappointed.

Marguerite, her heart greatly relieved by Blake's visit, for there was that in the manner of the man that gave her confidence, went to her own room and lay down.

She had had no sleep the night before. How could she sleep with such a load on her heart? Featherstone's promise had brought her no comfort. Indeed, the more she ·

thought over her meeting with him the more she regretted the impulse that led her to agree to his proposition.

She had been dreading the expedition that night, not for the danger there might be in it to herself, for she was driven to recklessness, but for the sake of Kohala. The more she reflected the stronger became her conviction that Featherstone was leading her into à trap. But the coming of Blake had given strength to her body and hope to her heart, if not rest to her mind, so that, without any idea of doing so, she dozed off, and was sleeping when Clem called her to dinner six hours afterward.

After dinner she tried to read, and failing in that, she took up her sewing—she always had some handy—and she kept at work till midnight.

She dressed for the street, putting on a warm wrap, for the damp nights of the Tropics are often chilly, and then, after extinguishing the boudoir light—the only one burning in the cottage—she went noiselessly out to the street.

Despite the comforting thought that Blake was near or watching her, her heart· fluttered so as she hurried on in the shadows that several times she was forced to stop for breath.

She reached the appointed place; but, to her relief, Featherstone was not there. She looked up and down the street, but there was not a living thing in sight.

After a wait of ten minutes, that seemed like as many tedious hours, Marguerite was startled by a step behind her and the loud breathing of a man in a hurry.

She turned, and by the light of. a gas lamp some distance down the street she saw the figure of some one near her, and she recognized the voice of the man she had been waiting for.

"Glad to see you have. come," was the salutation. "Will you take my arm? No? Very well, my lady; you may do better without. Now, keep close to me, or we may get parted in the darkness."

Although far from strong, Marguerite had the endurance and activity of far more robust women. His pace was quick and he breathed hard, like a man whose lips were set; but she kept close to him, neither speaking a word as they hurried along the unlit alleys.

At length they got beyond the city lights without being disturbed. About a mile up the Nuuanu Valley road Featherstone stopped and uttered a low whistle. It was answered by a whistle near by.

He whispered: "There is a carriage at hand."

They reached it and got in; but the carriage did not move. The hoarse voices of men were heard near by and the clicking of rifles, and one shouted out:

"Hold up there till we examine your load."

CHAPTER XXV.

IN THE DARKEST HOUR.

MARGUERITE heard the hoarse, peremptory challenge coming from the darkness without any feeling of alarm; indeed, it gave her courage, for she regarded it as an assurance that Blake was either near by, or else that the men with the rifles were acting under his orders. This remarkable man, with his quiet, earnest ways, his keen eyes and his power to read the thoughts of people—he had certainly read hers—had impressed her with confidence in his ability to do anything he undertook.

Once outside the guards, who he knew watched the principal roads leading into the city, Featherstone felt that he would be safe, for he had run the gauntlet with ease when there was more need for vigilance than now. But when he found himself halted he was, for the moment, so staggered that he could make no response.

Men who depend for success on cunning need to have ready wits. At heart Featherstone was a coward, but he had the manner that is apt to pass for pluck with the inexperienced.

Coughing, to give an outlet to his nervousness rather than to clear his throat, he called out, peremptorily:

"Hello, there!. Who are you?"

"Friends of Hawaii," came the response.

"Then you are friends of mine," said Featherstone, with affected joy.

"What is your name?" from the darkness.

"Captain Paul Featherstone, late of the English Army."

"And the lady who accompanies you?"

"Mrs.—Mrs. Marguerite Holmes. also English by birth."

"And Hawaiian by adoption," joined in the little woman. her voice strikingly musical in contrast with the hoarse tones of the man.

An approving laugh came from the darkness, and the sergeant of the guard asked:

"Have you a pass. Captain Featherstone?"

"I have not; I did not know one was needed. I am a subject of Her Majesty the Queen of England."

"If you were Her Majesty herself you could not go on without a pass."

"May I ask why not?"

"You may ask whatever you please."

"Then I demand to know why I am detained?"

" I am obeying orders."

"From whom?"

"The Provisional Government. Now, sir. let me ask where you are going this early morning with that lady?"

"To the Pali."

"Ah. that is a dangerous place in the daytime; it is a thousand times more so at night," said the sergeant.

"I was going to drive slowly on till daylight. Our purpose is to see the sun rise from the cliffs."

"Yes. that is a rare fine sight; but there is a good road up there and with your team you can make the trip from here in half an hour. I shall consult with the captain in charge of this district, and if he thinks it well to have you go on I shall let you off; but, for the lady's sake, not till I can see daylight on the crest of Lanihuli."

Featherstone choked down an oath. and the sergeant and his men held a whispered consultation, and some of them moved off; but enough remained back to form a post about the carriage, around which they paced with the quiet persistency that distinguishes soldiers on guard. Marguerite. though ordinarily impulsive and nervous, heard all this without a tremor of alarm. She was so well satisfied with the situation that she snuggled down in her corner with her shawl wrapped about her, and was actually dropping off into a doze when Featherstone bent over and whispered:

"Can you hear me?"

"I can," she responded.

"Do you know what I think?"

"How should I know?"

"I think you have betrayed me!" he hissed.

"How could I?"

"By arranging with these men to be here."

"I did not know you were coming here. You did not tell 'me. I have followed out your instructions to the letter, and if you have blundered again you should be man enough to place the blame where it belongs," said Marguerite, with a force that surprised him.

Hitherto he had regarded her as a sweet, cunning, weak, lovable little creature whom he had entirely under his control, and who would do his bidding like a trained dog; so that it hurt his inordinate vanity to find that the woman he had been regarding as his tool had set his authority at defiance and treated his assumed mastery with contempt.

He had been playing a bold game for large stakes, and he had shown a foresight and persistency that might have been regarded as able in a more commendable line. But now that he saw the chances for wealth vanishing it was, perhaps, natural that hate should spring from the ruins of his ambition and that he should look to revenge as the one thing that would appease his suffering.

Silence came again, but it brought him no repose. The tramping of the soldiers outside maddened him. The quiet, regular breathing of that amazing little creature in the corner, who must actually have dropped off to sleep, fell upon his ears with all the torture of the filing of a saw.

He turned and twisted and swore under his breath, all the while asking himself what he should do when daylight came and he was released. He could not well return to the city, and to go on to Pedro's would be to commit himself for the abduction of Kohala. He had had no thought of going to the Pali; but he told the

guards that that was his destination, and so there was
nothing left him but to keep good his word.   ?

Marguerite was entirely right when she inferred that
Blake was the man who held the carriage. She would
have known his quick, keen voic●had he spoken; but
as he did not, she concluded that he was not present;
yet he was.

After seeing that the carriage was properly guarded
Blake hurried back some distance to where a man was
holding a saddled horse by the roadside, and, after exchanging salutations, he mounted and rode back to
Honolulu.

He called at headquarters and found Colonel Loring
asleep on a sofa in his office. He woke him up and told
him what he had done, and, as to what he proposed
doing, he said :

"I am going to drive that carriage to the Pali."

"But Featherstone will recognize you," said the
colonel.

"No, he won't.".

"How can you help it?"

"He has a native driver now ; I know the man."

"Well?"

"I shall go to my quarters and make up like that
native. Trust me for that—"

"But how. can I help?"

"Mount twenty or thirty men as soon as it is daylight
and send them in all haste to Pedro's."

"To Pedro's !" exclaimed Loring.

"Pedro Molino, a Portuguese. He lives on the aban-
doned Markham place, to the left of the Nuuanu Valley."

"I remember. The fellow is a rascal."

"Yes, colonel, one of the grandest rascals in Hawaii,
unless it may be Featherstone. If there was a belt given
for pure cussedness and unadulterated villainy that fellow
would be entitled to one as big in girth as the Equator."

"And the woman, Blake, what do you think of her?"

"She's a daisy, colonel—a perfect gem of a woman."

"What!" laughed Colonel Loring, "has she caught
you, too?"

"She didn't try to. By Jinks ! like Captain Scott's

coon, I came down and surrendered without firing a shot. Any man hereafter who dares to say a word against that little lady in my presence must be a better man than me or he'll find himself badly licked."

"I shall keep that in mind, Blake; but on general principles I agree with you. Confound the cur, say I, who will slander a defenseless woman! What, are you off? Well, good luck to you, Blake, and depend on me to do as you request."

Colonel Loring rose, gave Blake a hearty handshake and saw him to the door.

When Blake got back to the carriage, which he did in the perfect disguise of a native, the first tints of the coming day were lighting up the stern, rocky head of Konahuanui, to the east of the Pali cliffs.

Without attracting Featherstone's notice, Blake, after having made himself known to his companions, who, though expecting the change, were amazed at its completeness, succeeded in removing the driver and in taking his place.

"Coming to the carriage door, the sergeant called in:

"Captain Featherstone, I have just received orders from the officer of the post to release you. Day is dawning, and if you hurry up you will be in plenty of time to catch, from the Pali, the sun coming up out of the sea."

Featherstone was in no mood to be grateful for his release; indeed, the soldier's words seemed to have on him a maddening effect, for he put his head out of the door and shouted to the man on the box:

"Drive on! Do you hear me! Drive on!"

"Where; to Pedro's?" came back the question in native accents.

"No, curse you! To the Pali! Don't you hear me?"

"Oh, I hear," was the quiet response.

"Then go."

"All right."

The whip cracked and the sleeping horses shook themselves and started off, a little stiffly at first, but soon they limbered into a smart trot.

Marguerite heard all this, but still pretended to be asleep. As the carriage swayed and turned in the ascent of the beautiful valley she caught frequent glimpses of the coming day on the crest of the steep volcanic hills to the right and left.

Her appreciation of the beautiful was intense. The glory of that Tropic morning so inspired her during the transformation from inky blackness to golden blaze of the sun on the mountain-tops that she forgot her troubles and her position.

Up through the sweet home-land of fair Koolau, up past the palm-thatched huts of the natives, up through the jungles of lantana covering the volcanic rocks the carriage rolled.

The man on the box, cheered no doubt by the glory of the scene, broke into a native song; but he had not finished the first verse before Featherstone, at some risk to himself, put out his head and shouted:

"Confound you! stop that noise."

"I make no noise; I sing," said the driver, and, to prove it, he went on with greater force, keeping time to the measure by cracking his long whip and stamping with his boots on the dashboard.

Marguerite heard all this, and had it been light enough Featherstone might have seen a roguish gleam in the long-lashed eyes and a smile playing about the sweet little mouth. What was torture to him she saw the ludicrous side of and heartily enjoyed.

They were within a few hundred yards of their destination, the Pali Cliff, over which King Kamehameha drove the last of his opponents into the sea, when Featherstone called to the driver to stop, which was promptly done.

"We must get out here, madam, and walk on," said Featherstone.

He sprang out, and extended his hands to help her; but she ignored his proffer of assistance and descended as lightly as if she were not stiff in every limb.

"Drive down the hill for a mile or so," said Featherstone to the man, who had descended from the box.

"Wait long, sa?" asked the man.

"I don't know. Do as you are told." Then, in the

same harsh voice, Featherstone turned to Marguerite and asked: "Can you make out without help?"

"I shall try to," she said, and as she could now see the road leading up to the top of the Pali, she sprang ahead.

CHAPTER XXVI.

WHAT MIGHT HAVE BEEN EXPECTED.

ALTHOUGH gentle and unsuspecting in his nature, and more ready to believe in the good in men than to suspect the wrong, Kohala, after that midnight meeting with Featherstone, saw into and through the fellow's character more clearly than if the wretch had made a confession in the presence of death.

He not only saw why Featherstone had clung to him abroad and followed him to Hawaii, but he inferred, with amazing accuracy, the part which the man had planned for Marguerite to act in the furtherance of his own schemes.

When he first heard Colonel Ellis's story—a story that reflected on Marguerite's honesty and fealty—love, jealous in proportion to its strength, maddened him, and he felt doubt of her in his heart, but he had too much pride to confess that doubt to his friend.

But when he recalled that she had given to him the best evidence of her love, that in the few whispered words they had apart after the marriage ceremony she warned him against the very dangers that now environed him, doubt gave way to a faith that filled him and thrilled him with confidence, and with a determination as to his own course of action, from which he had not and would not vary till death wrote "finis" to the close of the story of his own life.

He now saw why he had been brought here, and, while he was too loyal to the men of his own race to believe that they would scheme for his capture to aid the enterprise of Featherstone, he believed that Pedro and the captain had played upon their patriotism and made them their tools to gain their own ends.

Further, he realized—and the truth came to him like
a blow from a giant—that if Featherstone did not clearly
see the way to success he would not hesitate to put that
witness out of the way in order to save himself and to
silence the one witness whose evidence would crush him.

All this flashed through Kohala's mind as he stood by
the open window looking out into the impenetrable
darkness where he knew that guards were watching
to prevent his escape.

A high wind whistled through the plumy tops of the
palms and swayed the hissing undergrowth with a
sound like the dashing of the sea against the sides of
a moving ship.

This noise was favorable to the venture on which he
hastily decided. He took off his boots, tied them together
with a handkerchief and fastened them about his neck.

The fact that he had no arms intensified his caution.
The window opened on a piazza, and it was only a short
step from there to the ground. During the day he had
seen enough of the outside to give him some idea of
direction and of the immediate obstacles he might have
to encounter.

As it was so dark that he could not see the fingers
of his hand held close to his face, Kohala did not attempt to creep, but, standing erect and moving as si-
lently as a cat approaching its prey, he passed through
the window and out to the junglelike garden.

Glancing back, he saw the light in the room where
Pedro and his friends were drinking and consulting, and
this gave him a guide by which he could direct his course.
Before moving again he put on his boots.

Every few seconds he stopped and bent to listen, and
till he grew familiar with the sound of the wind away up
in the palms it seemed so much like the hoarse whispering of angered men that he could hear and feel the
thumping of his own heart.

As he went on, with many a backward glance, the light
in the window grew dimmer and dimmer, till it finally
faded out, and then he felt lost amid the tangle of lantana
and the walls of prickly cactus that seemed to rise up before him on every hand.

There is nothing so uncertain as the direction from which a sound comes in the dark, unless one is expecting it from a certain quarter. Over the whispering and hissing of the wind Kohala heard the barking of a number of curs. He knew they were near the house, but what direction that was in he could not tell.

While he was halted and listening he was startled at hearing, close by—so close, indeed, that it seemed he could smell the smoke-tainted breath of the speakers—two men in conversation. The first words that came to Kohala's ears were:

"Those fellows in there"—no doubt meaning Pedro and his friends—"are playing for big stakes; they'll make a fortune out of this, while we must be content with two dollars a day, ten cheroots and a pint of whisky."

"Well, don't kick, Sanchez; that is more than we were making before we took the job. My only fear is that it won't last long. Ah, if I had a good long head on me our positions would be changed, and Pedro would be guarding and I'd be planning to reap the harvest of gold. But I have an idea, friend Sanchez."

"You have?"

"Yes."

"Doesn't it astonish you, Tom?"

"I don't know. Why do you ask?"

"Well, an idea with you is so odd. But let us hear it before it goes."

"It is this, Sanchez—now you've got some sense."

"Is that the idea?"

"No, for you might have twice as much without being in danger of brain fever. But you know that everything's upside down in Hawaii at this time?"

"Everything but the Americans, Tom; they're up, and it strikes me they're going to stay up."

"Maybe; but you'll agree that they'd like to find the man we are guarding for two dollars a day, not to mention the cheroots and whisky."

"Yes, Tom, there is no doubt about that."

"And don't you think Colonel Loring would pay big to find him?"

"I am sure of it."

"Then, Sanchez, you can see my idea."
"Yes, but it's a bit foggy."
"Then I'll make it clearer."
"I wish you would."
"Let us carry off Kohala before daybreak."
"Where to?"
"Away from here to a point where one of us can guard him while the other one goes into Honolulu and sells his information and agrees to lead the soldiers to the man they want. There is a lot of money in that, and then it would save us from the trouble that is bound 'to come when Featherstone is hunted down, as he is sure to be. What do you think of the scheme, Sanchez?"

"Think, Tom? Why, I think you're what they call a genius, and I am in with you. Let us get closer to the house; it will soon be daylight and there is no time to lose."

The two men passed so close to Kohala that the arm of one actually brushed against him, and it was not till they had gone some distance, in what he now believed to be the direction from which the barking came, that he ventured to move on again.

"If they go back to examine my room," reasoned Kohala, "they will soon discover my absence, and then, as they cannot carry out their plan, they will try to get credit for discovering my flight and will give the alarm."

He pushed on with more speed, and had just reached an open space that he thought must be a road or a cleared field when he heard a series of appalling yells behind him, accompanied by the increased barking of the dogs and the discharge of firearms.

This startled him, but it did not lessen his presence of mind.

He knew that the uproar was intended to intimidate him if he were within hearing. This supposition was soon verified.

Above the clamor he heard Pedro's voice calling out:

"We see you! Come, there's no use trying to fool us! We don't want to harm you, but if you don't come back we'll kill you! Do you hear?"

If Pedro expected a reply to this, he was disappointed.

Again the shouting burst out; the flash of a lantern could be seen in the direction of the men, and the crashing noise of their tearing through the jungle drowned out the wind in the palms.

The lantern, without which Pedro could have made no headway, promised to be Kohala's salvation, for while it could not light up a path to liberty for himself, like the lighthouse beacon to the storm-tossed mariner, it indicated the place that was to be avoided.

The fugitive could only hold himself back by a strong effort of will. The impulse, as is ever the case, was to fly with all speed from the pursuing danger; but to have done this blindly would have been to exhaust himself before the time for the supreme effort came; and deliberately to control himself by such reasoning under such circumstances indicated a self-command of no ordinary order.

The open space reached by Kohala proved to be a road, and not a very good one at that; but whither it led he did not ask himself so long as it led him away from the men who were determined to recapture him, dead or alive.

As he ran on, reeling now and then into the lantana jungle on either hand, he stumbled over something and fell. In rising, his hand came into contact with a piece of wood that felt like a wagon-spoke, and without any reason at the moment he clung to it.

After this he had not proceeded more than a hundred yards when he heard the baying of a bloodhound—he had heard the deep, bell-like cry before and knew what it meant.

The animal seemed to be at his heels, and as he stopped to listen he caught the pounding of hoofs, showing that at least one of his pursuers was mounted, and he saw the swaying of the lantern.

Again Kohala's presence of mind—and he needed it at this juncture—did him good service. Under such circumstances the thoughts move with the rapidity of lightning and the reasoning, having in it the element of instinctive self-preservation, is usually right. If he ran till the dog came up his powers of resistance and defense would be lessened. · He realized this and forced himself

down to a quick walk, while momentarily the baying of
the hound came nearer and nearer.

Now the value of his find reconciled him to his fall,
and he came to regard it as Providential. As the hound
seemed to be right at his heels he halted and grasped his
club with a feeling of intense satisfaction.

He could not see, but the baying suddenly stopped, and
he felt the dirt thrown on his feet as the creature came
to a halt.

Setting his teeth and striking with all his might, in the
darkness, to be sure, yet with the almost certain feeling
that he was going to hit something, Kohala brought
down the club.

He felt it crashing into a pliant body. He heard a
gurgling groan, and he reasoned that for the present, at
least, there was no danger in that particular dog. ·

He had not long to wait, for the rider with the swinging lantern was coming on at a gallop and at this time
was not more than fifty yards away.

Now the fugitive put forth all his speed and shot ahead,
all the quicker for the slope of the ground which fell
away in the advance. ·

He did not see Pedro's horse suddenly stopping and
nearly unseating his rider as he came upon the huge dog
dying in the road; but he did hear the crack of a rifle
and the whizz of a bullet and the torrent of fierce impre-
cations which the now maddened and alarmed horseman
sent after him.

Kohala must have run fully a mile before he came to
a halt. Then the sounds behind had died out and the
wind had sunk to rest, or else there were no palms to be
whispered to. ·

As he stood trying to peer through the darkness he
saw before him, and seemingly high up in the heavens,
an opal glow on the rugged mountain crests above the
Pali.

He waited for some minutes, the hope in his heart increasing as the light of another day came creeping down
the mountains, driving the darkness and the mists before it. ·

Soon he began to recognize the hills; and not Tell,

when he escaped from an Austrian dungeon and found himself a free man amid the surrounding peaks and crags of his native Alps, felt the thrill that came to the heart of the young Hawaiian and sent the blood coursing joyously through his veins as he recognized the landmarks and mountain monuments above the historic cliffs of the Pali.

Lower and lower down the slopes came the light, revealing the outlines of the palms and bringing to view the nestlike huts of the natives.

Kohala hurried on, but still kept an eager lookout in every direction. At length he reached the Pali road, not twenty minutes' walk from the precipice.

While seated on a rock, resting and thinking, he heard, not far away, a native love-song, accompanied by the tramping of horses, the rolling of wheels and the cracking of a whip.

He recalled that it was not unusual for lovers of the sublime and beautiful—who were principally tourists—to come out to the Pali before day in order to see the great red disk of the sun lifting out of the eastern ocean and turning the turquoise waters to liquid flame. But who in troubled Honolulu at this time could give thought to the romantic ?

The panting horses came laboring up, and when the dim outline of a covered carriage came to view a hundred yards below, Kohala drew back into the lantana jungle and waited.

The carriage stopped before it got abreast of where he was and he heard voices; one was unmistakably that of Featherstone and the other was a woman's, and though he could not recognize it, it thrilled him and set his heart a-fluttering, for he could not see or think of a woman without having the idol in his heart leap up to his brain in the form of Marguerite.

He heard the carriage turning below, then the fall of feet and the sound of voices came nearer.

He parted the jungle and looked out; and his heart stopped beating for the moment as he saw his wife walking up to the cliff—walking up, clearly of her own volition, to the Pali, beside the man whom he knew to be an adventurer and a traitor.

Forgetting for the time where and what he was, the fires of jealousy blazed up in the young man's breast and he recalled what Colonel Ellis had told him in Hawaii.

That Featherstone should betray him was shocking, but he had never considered it among the impossibilities; but that the woman he had so worshiped should demonstrate her perfidy before his eyes was something so terrible that, as he realized it, he was stunned almost into insensibility.

They passed on, and then the reaction set in. The hot blood flamed from the young man's heart to his eyes till he looked like one of his own savage ancestors on the warpath. Choking down a cry of hate and rage he clutched his club, and, with the stealthy step of a tiger, followed his wife and Featherstone up to the Pali precipice.

CHAPTER XXVII.

ON THE PALI . CLIFFS.

It was a morning such as is never seen out of Hawaii, and not often there.

The valleys stretching away to Honolulu were veiled in a silvery mist, above which the fronded palms showed their heads like ships becalmed at sea.

A cloud in the upper sky looked to be changing from a warm opal to an intense golden flame, and it needed no stretch of the imagination to make it the sconce of the soft, warm illumination falling like a holy halo on the emerald land.

The mountains looked like masses of amethyst, tipped on their higher crests—which had already caught the sun—with giant points of amber and ruby that seemed to be self-luminous.

The air was still asleep, and through it floated birds and butterflies, the flash of their wings suggesting the opening and closing of animated blossoms.

If she knew that she were walking to death—and she was far from feeling that such was not now the case—Marguerite, with her keen sensibilities and poetic soul, could not have remained indifferent to the indescribable beauty and undreamed-of sublimity of her surroundings.

As she went on she could hear the fall of the breakers coming up, as it seemed to her, from the foundations of the volcanic hills like the measured beat—the rhythmic throbbing of the island's heart.

"If Kohala were only here, then death in such a place and at such a time could have no horrors." This she thought, as she, with daintier, airier step, went ahead of her panting, purple-faced companion.

Marguerite had been to the Pali before and with this same man, but it did not look like the same place. A glorious landscape, like an expressive face, has its moods and phases and its varying lights that give it a changing and ever-increasing beauty. Such a face and such a scene never pall, never weary the beholder with the oppression of soulless monotony.

At length she reached the crest of the cliff and drew back with a suppressed cry of alarm, for there yawned at her feet the awful precipice of the Pali, with the white breakers gleaming a thousand feet below like the flash of a cruel monster's teeth.

"Are you frightened?" asked Featherstone, with a mocking laugh, as he sat down on a red rock that looked as if it had been stained by the blood of the great kings slain.

"No," she managed to say, but she did not look at him. She stepped back with her gloved hand pressed to her eyes, as if to shut out the appalling abyss at her feet.

Strange that we can look up into the profound depths of space with no feeling of horror and that from the land we can look out on the destroying, all-devouring sea with no feeling of dread, while the nerves are unstrung by a glance from an upper window.

With the precipice out of sight, Marguerite ventured to look out and beyond. The east was all aflame, and the crescent of the rising sun, blood-red and burning, was rising over the far-off rim of the heaving ocean.

The circle of the barrier reef was visible, rolling like pearl mountains in whose liquid arms a thousand tangled rainbows had been caught and intermingled. So entranced was Marguerite with the transcendent glory of the scene spread out before her that she forgot everything but Kohala. His presence was the one thing needed to fill to overflow the chalice of her elevated and soulful rapture.

From the 'splendor of this waking dream she was aroused by the voice of Featherstone breaking in like a torturing discord on the entrancing flow of an exquisite harmony, and saying:

"You seem to enjoy it."

He rose from the rock, pushed his handkerchief into his pocket, as if he were provoked at it, and came and stood near her.

Before replying Marguerite turned and stepped back, with an instinctive desire to be out of his reach, and it may be, for the purpose of watching his face, in which she saw nothing reassuring.

"I have been enjoying it," she said.

"And I have spoiled the pleasure; is that it?"

He stooped and tried to look into her eyes; but without showing her dread—a dread increased by the proximity of that awful cliff—she avoided his gaze, and responded:

"You have brought me here, Captain Featherstone, now tell me your purpose."

"Oh, I shall do that. But first, let me ask: Did you not think I was going to take you to Kohala?"

"I did; but I now see the folly and weakness of my credulity, for you evidently had no such purpose in mind."

"Yet, madam, I assure you I had."

"Then why did you not carry it out?"

"Do you not know?"

"I do not."

"Then let me say I have been crediting you with more shrewdness than you seem to possess."

"I shall not ask why you have come to that conclusion."

"If you did I should tell you that you should have seen

that those dogs of guards—curse them! I wish I could see every man of them tumbling over the Pali—interfered with my plans. I could not go to Kohala without letting them know his whereabouts. · Do you understand that?" he sneered.

"I understand what you say." ·

"And I say what I mean."

"Then I must infer that you and your associate conspirators hold Kohala prisoner at some point not far from where we are?"

"I have not said that; but I will say that the man you call your husband is in danger of death—"

"Of death!" she cried.

"Ay, of death; and it will come swift and inexorable before another sun rises if you do not interfere to save him."

"If I do not interfere to save him?" she repeated. "Why, man, I am ready to die to save Kohala not only from death, but from suffering! For God's sake, take me to him at once!" and she clasped her hands and reached them out appealingly to him.

"Have a little patience—"

"But you torture me! Is it manly to do this?" ·

"Torture you! Torture you! Look at me, woman!" He drew himself up and smote his breast in a way that would have been mock heroic under any other circumstances, but which seemed tragic there. "Do you give thought to the torture you have brought to me?"

"If I have given you pain, pardon, for Heaven knows I never meant it; and it is the spirit of justice to measure the act by the motive that inspires it."

"Once your pleading would have been all-potent with me, for I loved you, and, loving you, I trusted you and believed in you as I never believed in a human being before. But you have betrayed me and shattered all the plans I had made for your happiness." He paused, bit his lip as if debating a second thought, and added: "But if you choose to do right, choose what you led me to believe you would do, it is not too late."

"I may have seemed to lend myself to your schemes," she said, a becoming flush rising to her usually pale cheeks and a brave light coming into the long-lashed gray eyes, "yet it was that I might the better understand you. I have never laid claims to a masculine intellect, yet I would have been an irresponsible and unreasoning idiot if I had closed my eyes to your purpose when you coaxed me to pretend love for Kohala after you had already asked me to be your wife."

"And you agreed to be my wife!" he interrupted.

"So I did. At that time I was poor and alone in the world, and although I knew that I did not and could not love you, yet I believed you to be a soldier and a gentleman whom I could, at least, respect. But I was not long in learning your true character, nor long in discovering that I could return Kohala's love. Then, for his sake, I acted my part; but from first to last I defy you or any one to say that I have done aught that any true woman would not have done under the same circumstances."

"Yes, you thought by throwing me over and marrying this gilded savage that you might become the queen consort of the King of Hawaii. Oh, I understand you," said Featherstone, with a mocking laugh.

"If I had had any such ambition then I must have doubted all your statements and among them your professions of love—the latter I never believed in, for I saw you wanted to use me simply as a tool for the furtherance of your mercenary designs. You told me that if Kohala married a white woman the natives would not only refuse to make him their king, but that they might seek his life. He did not want to be king; but he did love me and I loved him, and the world is wide enough for our love to live in beyond the shores of Hawaii," and she waved her hand to the east, from which came over the flashing waters the rising sea breeze.

Featherstone surveyed the slender figure with a look of unutterable hate in his bloodshot eyes. His fingers closed and opened with a murderous expression, and an onlooker would have said that it was to keep from seizing her at once and hurling her over the cliffs that he turned and walked down the slope for twenty yards, then came slowly back.

"Yes," he said, as he came and stood before her again,

"you have played a strong hand and won the odd trick. But it will do you no good. Your husband is a prisoner, and only death can release him—and you are here with me alone and helpless. Do you understand that, my lady?"

"I understand; yet I cannot think you so wholly a coward," she managed to say, "as to offer harm to a helpless woman."

"Coward! Fudge! I am not trying to establish in your eyes a reputation for gallantry."

He reached out his hand as if to seize her wrist, but she drew back with a startled cry.

Featherstone would have followed up this advance, but at that instant his quick ear caught the sound of a moving stone among the mass of rocks to the right.

He stopped and looked eagerly about him. The sun was now pouring a flood of gold into the Nuuanu Valley, and the silvery mists were rising and dissolving over the steeples of distant Honolulu.

What was that? Up from the valley, clear, resonant and startling, there came the thrilling notes of a military bugle, sounding the advance.

Featherstone looked eagerly down in the direction of the sound and caught the flash of the sun on polished arms. The soldiers were approaching, and his heart told him they were searching for him.

Driven to desperation by the thought that the end was nearing and that all his plans had melted into thin air, like the mists, he shot out an oath, and, springing back, caught the slender figure in his arms, and shouted:

"If we cannot live, we can at least die, together."

CHAPTER XXVIII.

A STRUGGLE FOR LIFE.

IT is said by those who have been suddenly confronted by what seemed death in its most terrible form that there is no sense of dread. Dread implies time for thought, a period during which the cause can be carried by a mental process to its effect; but in the face of immediate destruction, even though resistance be made, there is no sense of horror, for all the reasoning faculties are paralyzed.

Marguerite .sent up a cry when she saw Featherstone leaping toward her with the look of a madman in· his eyes; but entirely powerless. to move, she stood as if rooted to the spot.

She did not faint; but as he pressed her in his arms, still carrying her toward the Pali Cliff, he kissed her, and with her weak arms she fought him off as best she could, but he was entirely unconscious of the resistance she offered.

Curiously enough she noticed a crimson butterfly that at that moment flitted past her face; and she mentally appreciated its exquisite beauty, and recalled that, to the old Greeks, it typified Psyche, or the immortal soul.

She caught sight of the awful abyss, and the name in her heart burst up to her lips.

"Kohala! Kohala!"

"Ay, call upon Kohala; he is powerless to help you now!" shouted Featherstone, and he stooped to kiss her again.

Clear, high and. ringing, like a heaven-sent answer to the cry of Marguerite, she heard the loved voice answering:

"Kohala is here!"

With the swift sweep of an eagle, which with fierce cry rushes down on the despoiler of its eyrie, Kohala of Hawaii, from the rock behind which he had been con-.cealed, leaped straight at the throat of the traitor.

With his left hand fastened in the wretch's neck, in the right he swung the club that had already freed him from a nobler dog, and Featherstone staggered back, his hat severed by the blow and the blood flowing over his face.

He released his hold of Marguerite as he fell back, and in her amazement and utter helplessness she would have dropped to the ground had not other and more manly arms caught and sustained her.

"Marguerite! My life! my wife!" She heard the

dear voice of Kohala and felt his kisses raining on her face, then the heavens and the earth were blended and she knew no more.

"My Marguerite! my wife is dead!" cried Kohala, in tones of mingled rage and anguish.

He carried her back from the cliff, and, laying her down with her back against a protecting rock, supported the dear head with one hand and by means of his hat in the other he tried to fan her.

She had lost consciousness in that moment of supreme emotion and deadly peril; but, like a true defender of the loved, all his senses and powers were intensified.

From the instant he had freed his wife from Featherstone's clutch Kohala, in his anxiety for her safety, gave the fellow no thought, till the clicking of a pistol hammer recalled him to a sense of the true situation.

Springing to his feet and looking quickly about him, he saw Featherstone resting on one knee and covering him with a revolver.

Then came a flash and a crash. Kohala instinctively had leaped to one side and the bullet hit the rock above Marguerite's head, and the leaden splash struck one cheek and restored her to consciousness.

Featherstone was an adept with the pistol, but his hand was not steady and the blood from his wound had dimmed his sight.

He rose to his feet, with an oath at his failure, and was in the act of recocking the pistol when Kohala—not thinking of the club which had been cast aside—sprang at him, and, seizing the pistol, tried to wrench it from his grasp.

Featherstone, though not so tall as Kohala, was far more powerfully built, and, in his time, had prided himself on his athletic skill. In addition to this he had the Englishman's contempt for the strength and endurance of an opponent, particularly an opponent of another race.

He could not hold to the pistol and use all his great strength to advantage, so he threw the weapon to the front, and, as it went crashing against the jagged spikes of the Pali Cliff, the cartridges in the chamber were exploded.

"Curse you! now I have you!" roared Featherstone.
He threw his powerful arms about the younger man,
and so sudden and unexpected was the act that, before
Kohala could brace himself to resist, he was drawn at
least ten feet toward the abyss, which was now only a
few yards away.

Hate is strong, but love is stronger. Hate is for the
hour, but love is for eternity.

Kohala caught sight of the frightened eyes and white
face of his wife, and her helplessness filled him and
nerved him with the strength of a giant.

The one man was ponderous wrought-iron, the other
was well-tempered and elastic steel. The one man was
fighting for death, the other for life.

Featherstone felt two arms clasping his waist, while
the fingers, like the claws of a tiger, seemed to cut
through his flesh, and then he was lifted high above the
head of the younger man and flung back with a force
that must have crushed the life out of him on the rocks
had he not, with the instinct of a trained wrestler, clung
to the collar of his opponent, which, though it gave way,
broke the force of his fall.

Again Kohala's splendid presence of mind came into
play. He realized that he was standing between Featherstone and the brink of the Pali, and that he might be sent
over the cliff by the sudden onset of his panting assailant.
Quicker than it takes to record the act he had leaped beyond his foe and repossessed himself of his club, no small
advantage in such a struggle.

Featherstone saw all this as he sprang to his feet. He
was about to make another rush at Kohala, who, an-
ticipating it, stood on his guard, when another figure,
that seemed to have dropped from the sky, so sudden
was its appearance, leaped between the two.

In this figure Featherstone recognized the driver whom
he supposed to be with the horses down the hill, if, indeed, he had given him a thought since parting from
him.

"What brings you here? Back to your horses!" he
shouted, and he was amazed that the native did not fly
at his bidding.

"The horses are all right, captain."

This is what the native said, in the calm, impassive voice of a white man who was quite at home in such a scene and entirely able to take care of himself.

"Get away, you dog, or I will throw you over the cliff!" roared Featherstone, taking a step toward the intruder.

Instead of leaping back the driver drew a pistol from his blouse, pointed it in a businesslike way at the captain's head and said, in the same cool, maddening way:

"I wouldn't try that if I were you, Featherstone; you might get badly left on the contract. Ah, I see you think I am an ordinary Honolulu Kanaka driver. Well, I am not ashamed of your mistake, for some of them are good fellows, right up and down good fellows that you are not worthy to hold a candle to. There, you can now get some idea as to who I am, though I can't get the color off my face without water."

While saying this the driver divested himself of his blouse, loose cotton trousers and wig and stood before Featherstone in the uniform of the Provisional Army.

"Blake!" gasped the captain.

"That is my name, at your service."

"I am sold on all sides!"

"No, not sold; you have given yourself away; that's cheeper," and Blake laughed like a man enjoying the situation. Then, with a half-glance at Kohala, he added:

"You attend to the lady; I'll take care of this fellow."

Kohala sprang to Marguerite's side, knelt down and took the dear head on his breast.

"And what are you going to do with me?" asked Featherstone, with a defiant air and a backward step.

"What do you think should be done with you, come, now?"

"I know what you will not do."

"What is that?"

"Make me a prisoner."

"Oh, yes, I will; and let me say, Featherstone, that I will treat you kinder than you have treated your prisoners, and we'll give you a fair trial and a fitting sentence,

though there are men over in Honolulu at this time who
would lynch you off-hand, but Colonel Loring will not
permit that. Come, now, old fellow, save trouble by
surrendering, for you have reached the end of your
halter," and Blake took a forward step.

Featherstone took another backward step, and, with
an oath, shouted:

"I will never surrender!"

"Nonsense!"

"Keep back, I tell you!"

"Hold, man! Hold!" cried Blake. "Can't you see
the Pali is behind you? Come back!" and, for the first
time, he became excited at the awful danger threatening
the man in front.

At this juncture the blast of a bugle again rang up the
valley accompanied by the cheering of men and the
ringing of flying hoofs.

"I will not be taken, I tell you!"

"My God! Hold, man!"

Blake sprang forward as if to seize Featherstone, but
he was too late.

Featherstone reeled on the edge of the chasm, gave a
quick downward glance, tried to recover himself, then,
with a cry that froze the listeners with horror, plunged
over the precipice of the Pali.

"Come, Kohala, the Pali has lost its glory and its
beauty for to-day," said Blake, and, shading his eyes,
he tottered back from the chasm down which an unfortunate life had vanished.

"Devil though the man was," said Kohala, with a
shudder, "I would have saved him from that if I could."

"He brought it on himself. Sooner or later it had to
come. After all, what matters it whether such lives go
out on the gallows or over the Pali? Can I help you,
madam?"

"No, I thank you," said Marguerite, who now stood
trembling and clinging to her husband's arm.

"Then let us be moving."

As they went down toward the carriage Marguerite
slowly recovered from the awful shock, though it was
long before she was fully restored. It seemed to her as

if she had been and still was in a dream, and it was to satisfy herself that such was not the case that she said to Blake.

"Oh, sir, you have been so kind, and I have to thank you for so much." ·

"If I have been of use it was simply in the line of my duty; but I will say, madam, that I so admired your pluck and your genuine, no-mistake, fast-color love for your husband that I'd have looked on it as a pleasure to help you whether it was duty or not."

"Then I must thank you, too," joined in Kohala.

"Oh, that all goes for granted. But you must tell me your story as soon as we get a good chance. Featherstone was not in this job alone, and in the interest of justice we must get at the fellows who helped him. By the way, madam, were you alarmed when the carriage was stopped last night?"

"On the contrary, Mr. Blake," said Marguerite, "that incident brought me a great sense of comfort."

"Indeed!" with a pleased laugh. "How was that?"

"I knew that you had caused it."

"Good; so I did."

"But I never dreamed that you were the driver."

"No? Well, I thought I should surprise you before we got through. Hello! here's my team. And now, Kohala, if you and your wife will get in it will afford me the greatest pleasure of my life to drive you both back to Honolulu."

As Blake was holding open the door and Marguerite and Kohala were getting in a band of armed horsemen came on the scene, and when they learned what had happened they waved their hats, stood up in the stirrups and cheered to the echo.

CHAPTER XXIX.

A NEW DANGER.

BEFORE the carriage started off the officer in command of the mounted men said to Blake:

"You are right about that fellow Pedro."

"Did he confess?" asked Blake.

"No; but two of his men did."

"What have you done with them?"

"Sent the whole lot, except the girl, Annetta, prisoners into Honolulu."

"Good; now let us be getting back."

The horsemen fell in behind the carriage, and the hungry team never went down the valley road at such a pace before.

Residents in the Tropics are not early risers. The cool nights tempt to late hours, and so the people in Honolulu were not yet astir when the carriage halted before Marguerite's cottage.

As Kohala helped his wife out he said to Blake :

"I feel that it is an imposition to trouble you further, but I have a request to ask."

"And I am just in the humor to grant it," said Blake.

"When you have rested and had breakfast would you please call on Colonel Ellis, tell him all that has happened and say that I shall be here whenever he is ready to see me?"

"I shall be delighted. Congratulations on our success. Madam, good-morning."

Blake raised his hat, cracked the whip and was gone.

The couple were sitting in the boudoir about an hour after breakfast, Kohala eagerly awaiting the result of the mission intrusted to Blake, when they heard the roll of a rapidly driven carriage, which came to a sudden stop before the gate.

Unmindful of her warning or anxious to conciliate the new authority, Clem put in her head and said:

"If you please, mem and sir, there's a lady and a gent as wishes to see you."

"What are the names?" asked Kohala.

"Colonel Ellis, sir, and his daughter."

Kissing Marguerite again—that was the one act he could never weary of—Kohala went to the door.

He expected that his old guardian would be cold and provoked; great, then, was his joy when Alice kissed him as if he were her brother—indeed, she so regarded him—and the colonel took him in his arms and fairly hugged him.

"Well," cried Colonel Ellis, when he could get his
breath, "it strikes me that you have been getting up
a revolution on your own account. But where is the
lady? Your wife must be our friend. I tried—foolishly,
I now see—to direct the current of your wooing; I should
have known that love is the one irresistible, uncontrol-
lable force in Nature."

Alice looked at her father to see if she had his consent
to speak; and on receiving a meaning nod, she addressed
herself to the young husband and wife in this way:

"The Queen, who thought she was bringing about your
marriage to further her own ends, has not been successful. Through her friends the news of this marriage is
now flying over all the islands, and, as we may well believe, it will stir up a storm in Hawaii. We have discussed all this at home; and mother, who is still an
invalid—particularly in the forenoon—has sent me here
as her representative. Here are some of mother's orders,"
continued Alice, and she looked down at the palm of her
shapely right hand as if the orders were written thereon
and were plainly legible to herself. "We have a large
house and plenty of servants. That house is the home
of Kohala. There a welcome always awaits him. Kohala has 'gone and got married'—I don't know where I
first heard that colloquialism, but it suits. He loves his
wife, and we shall love her for his sake and for her
own. This is her home. Tell her to close up at once—
we'll send reliable people to pack up her belongings, and
so you fetch her with you to this house. These, my dear
Marguerite, are mother's orders; do you dare disobey
them?"

For reply, Marguerite came over and knelt beside Alice.
The two men, without waiting for further consent,
walked out, and, in order not to attract attention on
the now busy streets, they got into the carriage and
were driven round to the Hawaiian Hotel.

They found Phipps on guard at the door of the Council
chamber. The only person in the Council-room at this
early hour was Colonel Loring. So eager was the young
soldier to do his full duty and that nothing should fail by
his default that, when not engaged with his command

outside, he was always to be found at headquarters. • Indeed, as we have seen, he slept there.

"As there is no time to waste," said Colonel Ellis, when they were seated, "for the steamer for San Francisco sails to-morrow and the danger is hourly growing greater, I think it better that we should look the new danger in the face like men and see how it can be avoided or met."

"What danger do you refer to?" asked Kohala.

"Keona, ever since the birth of his daughter, has lived but for one object, and that was that he should one day see her the wife of the King of Hawaii. His hopes in that direction are blasted, and you should know the consequences — should have reasoned them out before you gave way to the promptings of your heart, though, mark you, Kohala, I am not blaming you. I think I should have acted, under the circumstances, about as you have," said the colonel.

"But what do you mean by the consequences?" asked Kohala.

"You should know without any asking. The natives believe that you, by this marriage, have betrayed them; and I tell you frankly that I fear for the consequences."

A knock at the door brought the conversation to a stop.

The door was opened by Phipps, and Blake entered, looking as fresh as if he had not been up and hard at work all night.

"What news, Blake?" asked Colonel Loring.

"The chief has just arrived, a score of armed men with him."

"Where are they now?"

"Still on board the steamer. But I should not be surprised if Keona appeared at any moment," said Blake.

"You must take my carriage and go with Kohala to the cottage, where you will find his wife and my daughter. Take the whole party round to my house at once," said Colonel Ellis.

Blake saluted, and, now keenly alive to the situation, Kohala followed him from the room.   •

CHAPTER XXX.

ALL FOR LOVE AND A KINGDOM WELL LOST.

BLAKE had come not a moment too soon with the news of the chief's arrival, and Kohala had left the Council chamber not a moment too soon for his own safety.

The two had not been gone four minutes when Phipps looked in and said:

"There's a man here who doesn't belong to the Council, and divil a wan of him knows the pass."

"And his name?" said Colonel Loring.

Before Phipps could put the question to the man outside a high-keyed voice called out:

"I am Keona of Hawaii!"

"Admit the gentleman," said Colonel Loring.

The door was opened and the chief, dressed like a white man, but with a repeating rifle in his hand, strode into the room.

"Glad to see you! When did you arrive?" was Colonel Ellis's salutation, as, with hand extended, he advanced to the chief.

"I have been betrayed!"

"Betrayed?" echoed the colonel.

"Yes, and you, Colonel Ellis, know it!"

"I, Colonel Ellis, know nothing of the kind; and let me say, right here, that I do not permit myself to be talked to in this way," said the colonel, hotly.

"I am Keona of Hawaii."

"I do not care, sir, if you are the King of Hawaii. I have ever been your friend, and I have done nothing to forfeit your regard or to merit this rudeness."

"Colonel Ellis, you are a man?"

"I hope so."

"And you have a daughter?"

"I have."

"What would you do to the man who betrayed her; to the man who was to have married her and then, like a dog, married another, and she a white woman?"

"The word 'betray' is the wrong word to use."

"It may be, for your speech is not mine."

"But you refer to Kohala?"

"I do."

"But would you want him to marry your daughter if he did not love her?"

"Love her?" repeated Keona, not at all understanding the proper meaning of the word. "Is not my Leila, with her youth and beauty and wealth—my Leila, who, since her infancy, has been betrothed to Kohala—more fit to be his wife than is this unknown white woman?"

"She may be, but that does not enter into the question."

"Why not?"

"Kohala is married."

"So I have heard, and may the curse of all the gods fall on him! But he lives, and he' is still in Hawaii."

"He lives," said the colonel, sternly, "and he is still in Honolulu; and he and his wife are guests in my house. You know that I was eager for Kohala to 'marry your daughter; but when he chose to marry another woman, and one who, in my opinion, is the equal of your daughter or mine, then I propose to stand by him. And let me say right here to your face, Keona of Hawaii, that if you attempt to harm this young man or his wife I shall forget our friendship and your wealth and your rank and I will see that you are treated like a common criminal."

"I shall do as my heart prompts," said Keona, with scorn; "and let me say to you that, though my race has melted away before yours, it has been through your vices and not on the batlefield. I do not fear the white man, and Kohala, the renegade, is white down deep to his heart!"

When the door had closed behind the chief Colonel Ellis turned to the young soldier and said:

"That man is desperate, Loring, and must be watched."

"I agree with you," said Loring.

"Can't you detail a number of men to keep a lookout on him?"

"I can, and I shall do it at once. Go to the house, and if you do not need Blake tell him to report here immediately." and Colonel Loring rang the bell for his orderly.

Colonel Ellis, feeling anything but like a man who was

going, that day, to give a wedding dinner at his own house, hastened home.

He found Kohala there with his wife, and they were as happy as if the last cloud had forever vanished from their lives.

The colonel saw this, and realizing that no good could come from telling them of the presence and the threats of the chief he refrained.

After dinner he took Kohala to the smoking-room and said:

"Tell your wife that you must both have your trunks ready for the steamer that sails to-morrow for San Francisco."

"But why this haste?" asked Kohala.

"You must ask no questions, but do as I say."

"Very well; but if I am to leave so soon I must go out and make arrangements with the bank about money."

"You must not be seen on the streets; I will attend to the money. I hold a balance of yours—more than you will need to spend for five years to come—and you can have more when you want it. My advice to you is to go to Europe or to Southern California with your wife. Get a home and keep house; never think of hotel life. After a while peace, prosperity and a better feeling will come to Hawaii, and then it will be quite safe for you to return with your wife. There, my boy, that is all I have to say."

"And from my heart I thank you for what you have said and what you have done," said Kohala, and he seized his guardian's strong, brown hand and kissed it.

It was not till the *Empress of the Seas* had been a day out from Honolulu that any one but Colonel Ellis and his family, Blake and Colonel Loring knew that Kohala and his wife had sailed for America.

Last March Alice Ellis became Mrs. Loring, and the valuable silver service that came on as a wedding present from America was sent by Kohala and his wife. The letter that accompanied it was written by Marguerite, and, among other things, it said:

"We are living in a perfect Eden to the east of Los

Angeles and not far from the Paradise of Pasadena.
But with Kohala ever near to assure me of his love,
the dullest, stormiest land on earth would be an Eden.

"We never weary of speaking of your great kindness
to us, and in that we forget the shadows that fell on us
in beautiful Hawaii.

"Life to me, up to this loving, was far from happy,
and I regarded it with indifference. Now every moment
is a joy, and I fervently thank God that I live and that
I may be worthy the continuance of this happiness.

"That you and your noble husband may be as happy
as myself and Kohala is the prayer of

"Your affectionate friend,   MARGUERITE."

THE END.

Where Is He Going?

Gentle reader, he is hurrying home.
And it's **house-cleaning** time, too
—think of that! Fifteen years ago,
he wouldn't have done it. Just at
this time, he'd be "taking to the
woods." But now, things are
different. His house is cleaned
with **Pearline**. That makes
house-cleaning easy. Easy for
those who do it—easy for those
who have it done. No hard work,
no wear and tear, no turmoil and
confusion, no time wasted, no tired
women, no homeless men. Every-
thing's done smoothly, quickly, quietly, an
easily. Try it and see.   331   JAMES PYLE, N.